Advance Praise for
THE COLOR OF SOUND

"*The Color of Sound* is a valentine to families everywhere. Isler explores multiple intergenerational relationships lovingly and honestly, while keeping a gifted and vulnerable girl firmly at the center. It's hard to imagine a book that I would want both my parents and my children to read, and yet, here is one."

—John Cho, *New York Times* bestselling author of *Troublemaker*

"A well-crafted, heartfelt, and affecting exploration of giftedness and the power of music to connect generations. Rosie's journey, as she struggles with her special talent and with how it defines her as both a family member and a friend, is one that will resonate deeply with many readers."

—Barbara Dee, author of *Maybe He Just Likes You* and *Unstuck*

"Rosie sees sounds as colors, and author Emily Barth Isler brings her story and characters to life with just as much vibrancy. This beautiful, intergenerational coming-of-age story about families, secrets, and self-discovery will stay with you long after you finish reading it."

—Gail Lerner, author of *The Big Dreams of Small Creatures*

"A heartwarming tale linking generations, music, Jewish culture, and the myriad challenges faced by tweens today, *The Color of Sound* is the perfect summer read, sure to become a perennial favorite."

—Joanne Levy, award-winning author of *Sorry for Your Loss*

"A deeply resonant story of finding your own song through the noise of everyone else's expectations. . . . This vivid and compassionate novel leaves the reader contemplating their own place in the world, in their family, and amidst the (violin) strings that connect us."

—Jimmy Matejek-Morris, author of *My Ex-Imaginary Friend* and *Forsooth*

"This bright, brilliant symphony of a story will play on in your head long after you've turned the last page. . . . Rosie's struggle with her family's expectations and its long history of trauma is deeply affecting and moving. I loved every beautiful, colorful, musical word."

—Sally J. Pla, author of *The Someday Birds*

"Music is vibrant color . . . dark history . . . and muted truth. This tale of connection, family, and generational secrets will tug on your heart as you root for Rosie to find her song and herself. A beautiful book of hope and acceptance."

—Elly Swartz, author of *Dear Student*

THE COLOR OF SOUND

Emily Barth Isler

CAROLRHODA BOOKS
MINNEAPOLIS

Carolrhoda Books®
An imprint of Lerner Publishing Group, Inc.
241 First Avenue North
Minneapolis, MN 55401 USA

For reading levels and more information, look up this title at www.lernerbooks.com.

Cover illustration by Jieting Chen.

Main body text set in Bembo Std.
Typeface provided by Monotype Typography.

Library of Congress Cataloging-in-Publication Data

Names: Isler, Emily Barth, author.
Title: The color of sound / Emily Barth Isler.
Description: Minneapolis, MN : Carolrhoda Books, [2024] | Audience: Ages 11–14. | Audience: Grades 4–6. | Summary: "Musical prodigy Rosie stops playing the violin, upsetting her ambitious mother but making room in her life for new experiences, including a glitch in space-time that lets her meet her mom as a twelve-year-old" —Provided by publisher.
Identifiers: LCCN 2023011571 (print) | LCCN 2023011572 (ebook) | ISBN 9781728487779 | ISBN 9798765612026 (epub)
Subjects: CYAC: Music—Fiction. | Mothers and daughters—Fiction. | Time travel—Fiction. | Synesthesia—Fiction. | BISAC: JUVENILE FICTION / Social Themes / Adolescence & Coming of Age
Classification: LCC PZ7.1.I874 Co 2024 (print) | LCC PZ7.1.I874 (ebook) | DDC [Fic]—dc23

LC record available at https://lccn.loc.gov/2023011571
LC ebook record available at https://lccn.loc.gov/2023011572

Manufactured in the United States of America
1-52928-51009-8/3/2023

For my parents, Andy and Toba Barth

CHAPTER 1

fugue: a piece of music with one or more
themes, each of which is repeated or echoed
by different instruments or voices

It's not simply that I dream in music. I dream the notes as textures and colors, as feelings and temperatures and tastes. When I wake up and try to write it down, what comes out are fragments of ideas that don't make much sense: lilies and velvet, sycamore trees, salt and butter, thick lines and thin wispy clouds, the smell of the first day of summer.

But I know how to play that when I take out my violin. It makes sense to me, like a code in a language only I speak, and I can translate it into melody. People have called me a "prodigy" or a "musical genius," but I've never known any other way to be. It's simply the way my brain works.

I haven't played the violin in sixty-seven days. My mother is calling it my music strike. She says that when I was a toddler, I went on a nursing strike; I refused to breastfeed for a few days, and then all of a sudden I was back, more ravenous than ever.

My music strike will not end like that. For one thing, how could I possibly have more passion for music than I did before? And for another thing, this isn't a battle of wills or a show of force. It's not even accurate to call it a music strike. I can't avoid music any more than I can avoid breathing. Music exists in all my other senses. It's in the smell of bread baking in the kitchen, in the colors of the budding tree outside my bedroom window. It's in the rhythm of how people speak, the sounds of cars driving past my house, the feel of fabric on my skin as I get dressed.

Music and I are inseparable. Just because I'm choosing not to share it with the world doesn't mean that music isn't still going on in me. Trying to stop it would be like trying to change my height or the shape of my face.

"Rosie," Mom says, her sea-storm tone breaking into the melody that constantly plays inside my mind. The gray sound makes me shiver.

"What?" I say, even though Mom hates when I

say "What" in response to a question. I should, she tells me quite often, say "Pardon?" or "I'm sorry, can you repeat the question?" if I think I've missed one.

Naturally this doesn't improve the color of her tone.

She's throwing various chopped vegetables into the salad bowl with an almost comical urgency. "Are you all packed, is what I asked."

I take silverware out of the drawer and put it on the center of the table. "Yes, all packed."

She pauses with the salad to catch my eye and give me a pointed look, sharp and shiny like steel. "Including your violin?"

There it is. A chess move in a match I didn't realize we were still playing.

"I'm not bringing it, Mom. I told you. I'm taking a break."

She scoffs, the sound like a puff of smoky fire coming out of her mouth. "You don't take breaks when you've made commitments. You have Mahler's Third in four months, plus the guest solo in Pittsburgh, the Symphony auditions—and I'm sure Peabody will want to see you again for next summer's concert."

I could've played this list on my violin like a

song, I've heard it said so many times. I know exactly what this strike will cost me, and I'm okay with it. But she isn't.

I could spend the next six weeks at the fancy, audition-only, just-for-prodigies music camp I'm supposed to be at already. I could focus on making my fingers match the notes painted in my brain so that the sound flows out of my bow, across the bridge of my violin, vibrating exactly four hundred and forty times for every A, four hundred and forty-six times for every B flat, and so on.

But I'm not at the music camp this year. I've been there the past four summers, and I wanted a break.

I *needed* a break.

This means that Mom has taken away my iPad and screen time. It also means that I have to go to Connecticut with her.

During dinner, Mom plays music. Mahler's Symphony no. 3—the one I'm supposed to play with the Philharmonic in a few months. She really never stops trying. What she doesn't understand, though, is that I don't even need to hear the music out loud to experience it. After hearing it once, I've already had every shade and brush stroke of it memorized and mapped in my head.

Dad won't be home in time to join us for dinner, even though it's our last night before Mom and I leave for six weeks. Dad will visit us up in Connecticut a few times, if and when his schedule permits.

My dad is a surgeon. He fixes people, and he tries regularly to fix me. He approaches my violin strike like it's a heart valve and he just cannot quite get the imaging right enough to make a plan for surgery. He asks questions like he's trying to find the hidden blockage or rupture, but I'm not a ventricle.

"Would you feel differently if you were being *paid* to play?" he asked recently. No, it's not about money.

"I bet if we put some of your concert videos up on social media, you'd go viral. Like those kids on TikTok! Would you like to be famous on TikTok?" Ew, no thank you.

"We could throw you a big party! And you could play violin for everyone. Would that be fun?"

It's like he's trying to bribe me but doesn't know me at all. Well, it's not *like* that. It *is* that. He's trying to bribe me and he doesn't know me at all.

I have zero interest in going viral or being famous. I don't want money or attention—at least not the kind of attention Dad has suggested.

Honestly, I'm just tired. During surgeries, Dad clamps peoples' arteries and veins to stop the flow of blood to their hearts while he fixes them. I wish I could clamp my brain off for a few weeks, to stem the constant flow of colors and thoughts and music and sound. I'd like to get a rest from it. This strike is as close as I can get.

♪

Mom plays more music in the car the next morning—Bach, Beethoven, Saint-Saëns. I sit in the back seat and drift in and out of vibrant technicolor dreams thanks to "The Swan" and "Für Elise."

The last time I played, sixty-eight days ago, it was spring. Now, the June sun beats down in the back of our station wagon and the calluses on my fingers are going soft, but I can still feel the music in my hands—how my fingers rest on the strings over the soundboard, how the bow feels in my other hand.

A different song pops into my head, one in bold cartoonish colors. It's "Over the River and Through the Woods," the song that little kids sing in elementary school.

To grandmother's house we go
The horse knows the way
To carry the sleigh
Through the white and drifting snow-oh

I guess kids who sing that song know the way to their grandmothers' houses. Over the river and through the woods.

I don't know the way to my grandparents' house. Not that I need to—I mean, my mom is driving, and I'm only twelve. But I don't recognize any part of the drive. It's the opposite of how my hands know the music I'm hearing from the car speakers. And there's a good reason for this. We don't see my grandparents a lot.

"So what are your plans, Rosie?"

Mom's voice cuts into my thoughts, the boldest of blue in a laser-thin line. For a moment it even drowns out the steady brown hum of the SUV's movement.

"My plans?" Apparently we're in the middle of a conversation, but I was not aware.

Mom sighs. "For the summer. While we're staying with your grandparents. What are you going to do with your time, if you're not playing the violin?

Remember, tech is off the table—no phone, no computers, no iPad. So what are you going to do?"

This is the big question, isn't it? When I first went on strike, I still had school. I put all my energy into homework and extra credit and trying not to look like a total loser with no friends. I even made a list: *Things Normal Kids Do All the Time That I've Never Had Time to Do Because I Was Playing the Violin or Listening to Violin Music or Thinking about the Violin.* Everything on that list was inspired by TV shows I've seen and books I've read. Set up a lemonade stand. Have a crush on someone. Get a phone. Watch YouTube videos of random stuff. Do arts and crafts. Sneak out (where?) with friends (who???). Go to a party (hahaha).

I have no idea where to begin, and without even Julianne in my life, it all seems impossible and pointless. Even now, I can still picture Julianne's face that day we had our fight—and the Monday afterward, when I watched her sit with Isabela and Amelia at lunch. I have to stop thinking about it before my eyes fill with tears.

"I'll figure it out when we get there," I say now.

Mom frowns, our eyes meeting briefly via the rearview mirror, but she doesn't say anything more.

I must drift off to sleep, because the next thing I know, we're under a dappled canopy of green leaves, with walls of gray rock on either side of us, winding up a country road that might be familiar.

"We're about six minutes away," Mom says softly when she sees that I'm awake.

I close my eyes, letting the car lurch me this way and that way as the road curves. When I open them again, I see more green, more stone walls, and large houses down gated driveways.

"Is there anything you want to ask me about Grandma Florence before we get there?" Mom asks. There's a hitch in her voice, as if it's a broken line, warning-yellow like the strip down the center of the road we're on.

I shake my head—and also say, "No," because she's looking at the road and not at me in the mirror. I suspect she waited this long to invite questions because she doesn't really want to answer any. And I wouldn't even know where to start.

Here's what I do know about Grandma Florence. She's had Alzheimer's disease for the past seven years, which means I barely remember her from before dementia set in. She was confused and quiet the handful of times I've seen her since then. She's a tiny lady, short and rail-thin, with wavy white hair cut above her shoulders and big round glasses. I know she's Mom's mother. That she's married to Grandpa Jack, Mom's father, who's the same age as Grandma Florence—seventy-eight—but is healthy and active, and quiet in a very different way.

I know that Mom grew up here, at this house we're approaching. I know she left home when she started college and hasn't spent much time with her parents since then—not even after I was born and she quit working outside of the home.

I know that Grandma Florence is getting sicker, which is why we're going to visit. I know she's in bed all the time. I know she can barely speak, and no one is sure how much she can understand when people speak to her. I know I'm dreading seeing her because I don't want to think about anyone being so sick. I know she won't know who I am.

I don't know who I am either. Now that I'm not playing the violin, I feel like a piece of my body is missing.

The car slows and Mom puts on her blinker, turning left into a driveway with an automatic white gate that swings open for us. She waits until it's fully open before driving through and pausing to watch it slowly swing closed behind us. She inches down the driveway as if she doesn't want to actually arrive.

Ahead of us is the white house with green trim. The two levels and attached garage are weathered but beautiful. The house is huge, made up of non-matching sections my grandparents added on at various times in the almost fifty years they've lived here. Mom will be staying in the newest addition on the ground floor, while I'll stay upstairs in her old bedroom.

Surrounding the house is a big patch of land, much bigger than any yard in our neighborhood. The long driveway splits off in two directions, one path leading up to the house and one looping behind it around the edge of the property, disappearing from view. Somewhere behind the house there's a fancy pool that Grandpa Jack added after he sold his company for a lot of money. I'm fuzzy on the details, but I know that when Mom was young, my grandparents had very little money, and things changed drastically for them around the time she finished college. Of course, no one talks about this—no one talks about much of anything in my family, at least not to me—but I've picked up clues from listening to Mom video chat with my aunt Lily.

Mom parks on the curved driveway right in front of the house. I look around as we get out, half expecting Grandpa Jack to come over and greet us. But the only thing I see that's moving is the gigantic dog that bounds toward the car.

"Of course," Mom mutters, rolling her eyes briefly. "The dog."

Vienna barks and heads straight for me. I cower closer to the car because I know she could topple me over. Still, out of some polite instinct and against my better judgment, I hold out a hand to her. She slows as she reaches it, pausing to smell me.

Vienna is a Bernese mountain dog, and she definitely weighs more than I do. She comes up to my chest, her panting loud and turquoise with delight at new things to smell. I'm tempted to crawl back into the car just to get away from her, but I don't want to offend Grandpa Jack if he happens to be watching from inside. The various dogs my grandparents have had over the years have always been a point of tension between them and Mom; she seems to dislike them even more than I do. But I don't want to turn this into a big deal. If I'm going to be here all summer, I'll have to figure out how to live with Vienna.

I take a deep breath and pat her on the head gingerly. Her thick black fur is coarse, and I can smell her breath, brown and stale and moist.

"You go on inside," Mom tells me. "I'm right behind you—just bringing a few things in right away. We'll come back for the rest later."

Vienna follows me as I walk up the two green-painted steps to the elegant front portico with pillars on either side.

The door is unlocked and I push it open. I'm immediately hit with a smell I'd know anywhere—a song I have memorized, even though I've only been here a few times. It's musty carpets and cinnamon cake and old books and empty fireplaces and freshly cut grass and exposed beams and Vienna the dog. It's sweet but in a minor key, full of deep reds and dark browns and rich bass notes.

Mom steps in, closing the front door behind us. She places a few things out of sight in the foyer around the corner to my left.

"We're here," she singsongs. "Dad? It's me, Shoshanna. And Rosie."

I follow Mom to the right, past the staircase and through a little hallway to a formal dining room. Vienna trails me like I have roast beef—or whatever dogs love to smell—in my pockets. She makes me very, very uncomfortable, that dog.

Grandpa Jack comes into the dining room through the door on the opposite side. He must've been snoozing because his tuft of white hair is mussed and his shirt is rumpled, and he seems kind of surprised to see us.

"You made it," he says, holding out his arms. I'm not sure which one of us is supposed to run into them, but it doesn't matter because Vienna beats us to it. She leaps up onto Grandpa Jack as if she's the one who hasn't seen him in over a year.

"Down, girl," he says to the dog, and she sits, wagging her ginormous tail across the rug that covers most of the floor. Mom always says rugs like this are more valuable if they've got threadbare patches and discolorations, which makes absolutely zero sense to me. But this particular rug must be especially valuable because it's been worn bare in several spots. I have to imagine Vienna had something to do with that.

In books and movies, grandparents are always obsessed with their grandchildren, but Grandpa Jack can't take his eyes off Mom. He looks at her like he's seeing her for the first time and also like he can see every version of her from the past forty-something years.

"Hi, Dad," she says, stepping into his hug. Her back is to me, and over her shoulder I can see Grandpa Jack's eyes close softly.

When Mom steps away, I wave awkwardly to Grandpa Jack. He nods at me, as if he's also unsure how we're supposed to greet each other.

"Rosie," he says. "Welcome. So glad you're here." Grandpa is a little taller than Mom, with thin arms and a rounded stomach. Most of his wrinkles sit in areas that suggest they're smile-induced, which is something I like about him. His voice complements his light blue eyes—it's a slightly darker blue, but almost as glass-like and shiny. Every time I've seen him, I've had the same thought: I wish I knew more about him.

Honestly, we've never spent more than a day or two at a time together, thanks to my schedule of rehearsals and lessons and concerts—and Grandma Florence's poor health. Now it's fully hitting me that we're about to spend six weeks together.

I can imagine that after years of living in this house with only Grandma Florence, having Mom and me here is going to be quite a change for Grandpa Jack.

Mom looks around, taking in the room. Sunlight streams through the thick window glass, blocked in places by ceramic vases and decorative colored-glass bottles, sweeping over the oblong table and its ten chairs, the dust on the wooden sideboard, and the paintings on the walls. "Where's Mom?" she asks.

The smile doesn't leave Grandpa Jack's lips, but when he speaks, his voice is a heavy jade green. "Upstairs, of course," he says, gesturing behind us.

Mom has already told me that Grandma Florence has been getting worse lately—that she "doesn't have much longer." I hate that euphemism because it's so vague. She's dying. We know that. But no one can give me a sense of the actual timing. Six months from now? A year?

We follow Grandpa Jack up the dark wooden staircase and down a long hall. "There's your room, Rosie," he says, gesturing to an open doorway as we pass it. "And I'm in here these days," he adds with a nod to the door across the hall. "We've got the visiting nurse coming every morning, but I like to be close by the rest of the time . . ."

We reach the main bedroom. As soon as I see Grandma Florence in the king-sized bed, looking so tiny and shrunken, staring off in the middle distance as if she has no idea where she is, I know: she's going to die *soon*.

Grandpa Jack taps lightly on the door, more staccato than a trill, using the knuckles of his right middle and ring fingers. "The girls are here, Florence," he says loudly.

Grandma Florence's gaze doesn't leave the empty center of the room, but she smiles. "The girls? Is it Lily?"

Mom shoots Grandpa Jack a look. "Not Lily," she says, stepping closer to the bed. "It's me, Shoshanna. Remember? Lily lives far away and never visits you. But I do! And I brought Rosie."

"Where's Lily?"

Grandpa Jack clears his throat, a noise of clashing colors—ochre and puce mixing to an unpleasant shade. "Lily lives far away," he says patiently, and I can tell they have this conversation a lot. I've certainly heard Mom complain to Dad about Aunt Lily—about how she's so obsessed with the past and how she can't get herself "organized" to come see her family enough. I've only met Aunt Lily five or six times in my life, but I haven't seen my grandparents much more than that, so I'm not sure how fair Mom's criticisms are.

"Isn't Lily in school?" Grandma Florence asks.

Grandpa Jack shakes his head. "No, she's an adult. She lives in Austria. Shoshanna is here, though."

I'm wondering if we'll need to explain that my mom is a grown-up, that she lives in Baltimore with my dad, that she has a daughter (me), and all sorts of other details. But Grandma Florence's face brightens and she snaps her eyes away from the blur of nothingness, straight into my line of sight.

"Rosie," she says, her voice pink-satin dreamy. "With the violin."

"No," I say, sounding far more metallic and harsh than I planned. "No violin. Just Rosie."

Grandma Florence looks confused again. "What happened to the music?"

"No, Mom, you were right!" Mom jumps in. "It's Rosie with the violin. She just . . . doesn't have it at the moment. It's downstairs."

"No, it's not," I hiss at Mom, already afraid of her reply.

"Yes, it is," she says through gritted teeth. "I packed it in case you change your mind, and I brought it inside first thing because you know it can get so hot in the car . . ."

That's all it takes to make me turn on my heel.

The background music that plays in my head almost constantly has turned to an angry red buzzing, and I can hardly see through the burgundy haze.

"Excuse me," I wheeze as I push past Grandpa Jack and down the hallway.

I know Mom is following me even before I hear her speak.

"You didn't think I'd leave your violin at home, did you?" she says. "You know it needs to be temperature controlled. How would we make sure it stays perfectly humidified for six weeks if we left—"

"It's not that," I say, whirling around to face her in the doorway of her childhood bedroom.

"Well, if it's not that—"

"Don't you see what I mean now?"

She looks genuinely surprised; a vacant, confused look crosses her face. I pull her into her old room and close the door, even though I know Grandpa Jack's hearing is bad and Grandma Florence has no idea what's going on.

Mom's old bedroom contains no trace of the kid she must've been once. Its two twin beds, bare walls, and plush white carpet might as well have come straight out of a hotel.

"This is exactly why I am not playing the violin right now," I say, my hands on my hips and my voice a clangorous discord. "Grandma Florence can't remember who you are or that Aunt Lily lives in Austria, but she can still remember that I'm 'the one with the violin,' right?"

Mom frowns, still at a loss.

"That's the problem!" My voice becomes a thick river of murky blue, and I try not to cry. "That's all I am to everyone. The girl with the violin."

I can practically see the wheels turning in Mom's brain, as if she can reshape my ideas into a different story. "No, honey, she has Alzheimer's, she just can't remember all the other things—"

"There *are* no other things about me!" I explode. "That's *the* thing. The only thing. And that's the problem!"

From the hallway, Grandpa Jack calls, "Is everything okay?"

I look down at the carpet, at my shoes sinking into the plush strands. Mom excuses herself to go out and talk to Grandpa Jack. I'm sure she'll spin some lie, like "Rosie's just hungry" or "Rosie gets carsick and it makes her grumpy," to explain away my rudeness and yelling.

I walk over to one of the beds and flop down, straight like a wooden board, my face hitting the pillow with a *thunk*.

I want to scream into it, but apparently Grandpa Jack's hearing is better than I thought it was.

CHAPTER 2

divertimento: a piece of music written
for entertainment, usually light and
somewhat upbeat

My mother says there is exactly one right way—
and a million wrong ways—to do basically
anything. Family size: Parents should have only one
child so they can focus all their energy on that child.
Food: If you don't make it at home, you shouldn't
eat it. Pets: Why bother? They're not human. And
see above, re: children—you should focus all your
attention on your child. Birthdays: Should be in
the spring. That's the best/only time to be born.
Books: The greats have already been written. Music:
Classical, obviously.

That's just a sampling. As for me, I have other
ideas. For example, I think it would've been nice to

have a sibling. But since Mom's only sibling, Aunt Lily, has lived in Europe since Mom was in high school, and Dad is an only child, I guess they didn't really see the value. I would've liked to have a little sibling. It would've taken some of the pressure off me.

"Children should play outside" is another one of those pronouncements Mom likes to make, her words like the trumpet solo in the middle of Mahler's Symphony no. 5. Usually it makes me laugh, because I've rarely played outside. I have violin lessons or rehearsals or concerts practically every moment of the day, and also I'm twelve now, which is past the prime age for that sort of thing.

But as we're eating lunch on our first day in Hawthorne, Connecticut, Mom advises me to spend the afternoon outdoors. And what's my alternative? I've skipped out on camp, I'm not playing the violin, I'm self-conscious around Grandpa Jack after my outburst earlier today, and the last thing I want to do is spend time with Mom.

Lunch is casual but awkward. Tamar, the housekeeper who helps out a few times a week, keeps the fridge stocked, so Grandpa and Mom and I make sandwiches out of cold cuts and other prepared food.

We sit mostly in silence at the grand dining table. Mom has tried to start a few conversations about "safe" topics: the weather, the food, more weather. But Grandpa Jack doesn't seem interested in talking. He's wearing his hearing aids, so I know he can hear her. He just keeps looking out the window or staring down at his food. As soon as he finishes his roast beef sandwich, he takes his plate and some food containers back to the kitchen.

What a lonely, solo life he has here, I think as I watch him lope quietly away. He and Grandma Florence were once a duet; now she's mostly silent. Back when Mom and Aunt Lily were growing up, I suppose their family was a busy rotation of sound—a Baroque string quartet like the one I played in at camp last summer, made up of two violins, a viola, and a cello. But gradually, everyone has left or gone quiet, the music dwindling to a lone melody.

Of course, he's got Tamar around, and the nurse, and probably someone who takes care of the lawn and stuff. And Vienna, which I guess must be comforting to somebody who actually likes dogs.

Mom and I gather the remaining dishes and bring them to the kitchen. She says, "I'll give everything a quick rinse before I put it in the dishwasher. Then

I have to go upstairs to give Grandma Florence a bath—the nurse is only bathing her every other day and I want her bathed daily. And I have to remember to call her doctor back . . ."

I watch as she moves between the fridge and the kitchen sink, her soft shoes quietly thumping on the ceramic tile of the floor. The rhythm makes me think of a metronome, steady and unwavering. I'm not a fan of metronomes, though I'm used to conductors using them to keep time. Music should have rhythm, of course, but like a human being, it should be allowed to move and breathe.

I have the impulse to help her with the dishes, but Mom's never wanted me to waste time on chores when I could be practicing.

Except I'm not practicing now, and I have no idea what to do with myself.

As if she's read my mind, Mom says, "You go take a walk around the property. Do some exploring."

"What should I . . . look for?" I ask, biting my bottom lip.

Mom puts a hand on her hip. "Honestly, Rosie, I shouldn't have to explain to you how to entertain yourself for a few hours without the internet. Just enjoy the fresh air."

I'm pretty offended that she thinks it's "the internet" and not the violin that's left me incapable of entertaining myself. "Is that what you did when you were a kid?" I say sarcastically.

She doesn't miss a beat. "Yes. Your grandparents have a lot of land. Just don't go in the pool by yourself, and be back by five for dinner."

She leaves the room before I have a chance to argue.

If I go through the dining room and turn left, instead of to the right and into the kitchen, there's the living room with its itchy cream-colored couch and several upholstered chairs facing the fireplace. It's uncomfortably formal aside from the shelves full of old photo albums. Opposite the fireplace is a door, in front of which Vienna is sprawled out, snoring loudly. I tiptoe past her, hoping not to wake her.

Beyond the living room is a room made almost entirely of glass, with double doors that lead out onto a gray stone terrace. I remember this glass room and the terrace from previous visits. They face west and offer the most spectacular view of the sunsets. As I enter the now-quiet room, I remember those gorgeous ribbons of orange, pink, and red that rever-berated into it the last time I was here, listening to the sun make its descent into the hillside.

Outside the glass sunroom, beyond the terrace, is a patch of grass so vast I guess it should be called a field, not a patch. It stretches so far off into the distance that it blends into the horizon, like the ocean does at the beach. It's framed on both sides by a dense stretch of trees. And at the far left side of the field, at the edge of the woods, there's a small cabin.

I don't set out to walk to it, but something's pulling me there, like the gentle force of a bridge between verse and chorus. As I get closer, I see it's more of a shed than a cabin. Instinctively, I put a hand on the rough wood siding. It's warm from the sun, vibrating a major chord in my eyes. I let my hand drift across the wood as I make my way around to the front of the shed, where there's a door. It isn't locked, and I'm drawn by an urge to go inside.

I push the door open with a silver *glissando* of a creak, the sound sliding lightly from one pitch to another.

And I realize someone else is already in there.

The person—a girl—turns around. It's dark in the shed, and I can't make out her facial features.

I can only see that she's shorter than me and her hair is dark like mine.

"Who are you?" she asks, her words a dark, deep red, and sharp as sticks.

The door has shut behind me and this girl and I are alone, alone, alone, far from anyone else who could hear me if she hurt me.

"Who are *you*?" I ask back, trying to make my words as red as hers, to scare her the same way she's frightened me.

The girl steps closer. "I asked you first."

"Well, I asked you . . . second." I hear how ridiculous it is as soon as I say it. A laugh escapes my lips.

The girl laughs too, and I relax a bit. As my eyes adjust and I take in her face, I get the sense that I've seen her before, though I can't put my finger on where.

"I'm sorry," I say. "I just wasn't expecting to find anyone else in here . . ." I suddenly realize that this girl is my first—and possibly only—potential friend for this summer. Who am I to send her away just because this shed is technically on my grandparents' property? Maybe this girl—the daughter of a neighbor, probably?—has been hanging out in here for months. Maybe she thinks *I'm* the trespasser.

I grasp for the first convenient lie I can think of, a thought hanging in the air like a strand of gold. "I just came here to get out of the sun for a minute," I say.

The girl raises her eyebrows at me. There's a twinkle in her eye—not quite mischief, but something close to it, something fun-seeking and adventurous. She sparkles blue and green and teal.

"You don't have to make up excuses," she says. "It's fine that you're here."

"It's not an excuse," I say reflexively, even though the girl just told me it doesn't matter.

She gives a knowing eye roll, but I don't feel like she's making fun of me. I can see now that she has huge brown eyes and her hair is in messy, frizzy curls, kind of like mine would be if I didn't know how to properly take care of it.

"What's your name?" she asks.

I'm not sure what compels me to tell her the whole thing, but I find myself saying, "Golden. My first name is Golden, but everyone calls me by my middle name, which is Rose. Call me Rosie, please. I know, it's weird . . ." I trail off, but she's looking at me like I've said something magical.

"It's not weird at all! It's a beautiful name. I love

names like that—like where someone goes by their middle name or has an unusual nickname or something. It's so mysterious!"

I laugh again. Her enthusiasm is kind of sweet. I like her. Something about her, though, just feels so . . . familiar.

"What did you say your name is?" I ask her, taking another step toward the center of the shed, trying to get the smell of musty wood off my tongue and out of my ears by breathing through my mouth.

"I didn't," she says, "but it's Shoshanna."

I freeze. "It's *what* now?"

The girl laughs. "Shoshanna. It's Hebrew. Actually, it means *rose*, like your middle name. But you can call me Shanna."

Now I'm really reeling. All at once I know why the girl looks familiar. She looks like she's right out of a photograph—the kind my parents told me they used to take with film and have developed at the pharmacy, that my grandparents have in albums. It's because she looks exactly like my mom did when she was my age, and she has Mom's name too.

"Hi," I say, still stunned.

I start working out the possibilities in my head. Maybe Shanna is Aunt Lily's secret daughter who secretly lives here? And maybe that's why this girl looks like Mom did at this age, and maybe her mother—my aunt—named her after Mom? But Jews don't name their babies after living people. And Lily lives in Austria—I know that for sure. Mom video chats with her once every few weeks, and Aunt Lily regularly sends me postcards and little gifts from Europe. If she had a daughter, we'd know about it.

My thoughts feel thick like molasses, and I sink to the floor to sit with my legs folded. None of this makes sense. I try to keep my breaths steady and my body still.

"Sorry," I say to Shanna, who's watching me curiously. "I'm just . . . You remind me so much of someone. Can I—Are you . . ." I don't even know what to ask her. *Are you possibly my cousin who I know doesn't exist? Are you a ghost? Are you real? Am I dreaming?*

Something deep inside tells me I'm not dreaming. So I decide to test out the next theory that springs to mind.

"Silly question," I say, looking at Shanna, who sits down a few feet from me. "What . . . what year is it? I know it's weird to ask, but I'm doing this, uh, experiment . . . for school?"

Shanna blinks at me. "In the summertime?"

"Yeah, I go to this really weird, intense school. We have, um, projects over the summer. And I'm doing this one about"—I think fast—"about the way people *say* what year it is. Like, how you say the numbers, you know?"

Shanna gives me an *ummm, okay* look and answers in a fake British accent. "It's the year nineteen hundred and ninety-four, my lady."

I gasp.

"Just playing with you. I say it 'nineteen ninety-four.' Why, do some people really say 'nineteen hundred ninety-four'? Or, like, 'the year ninety-four,' without the 'nineteen?' Is that what your project is about?"

I stare at her, my vision like a black tunnel focused on her face. All I see are her eyes, so much like my own that I can't blink. I nod, relieved that she's given me a way to continue this conversation. She's bought my lie and built on top of it.

"Right," I say, trying to sound casual and serenely blue, "something like that. I'm also really . . . into names." Now I'm trying to sound *super* casual, like light blue, even softer and gentler. "What are your parents' names?"

"Florence and Jack."

Could this be a prank? But who would even do that? And why?

"I love how we have this floral thing going—my mom and I, and my sister's name is Lily, and now I've met someone named Rose. Isn't that funny?"

I let the gasp I've been holding in come out as a laugh and just say, "Yeah."

I'm talking to my mom. I'm somehow, magically, impossibly talking to a twelve-year-old version of my own mom. But she's . . .

Not only is this person the wrong age, she's also sparkling and effervescent in a way my actual mother is not, with bold colors and pastels in the same key. Shanna is funny and cheerful, and we've already had more of a real conversation than I've ever had with Mom.

"How old are you?" I ask.

"Twelve," she says. "And a quarter."

I nod slowly. "I just turned twelve."

"Seventh grade?"

I nod. "In the fall."

"Me too."

"And it's nineteen ninety-four, you say?" I ask, staring at Shanna. Have I traveled back in time? Or has she traveled forward? Or is this all in my head?

She shrugs. "Yeah, that's how I say it. What a funny project. What school did you say you go to?" She inches closer to me, and I can see a little scar on her left knee, just like the faint one my mom still has.

Maybe this is my punishment for my music strike. My mom has gone back in time to . . . teach me a lesson?

Nope. That's not how things work.

I shove these thoughts away and focus on Shanna. "I go to school near Baltimore. I'm just here this summer to visit my—"

But I stop short. If I say, *I'm just here this summer to visit my grandma Florence and my grandpa Jack*, well, that's going to raise some suspicions. And somehow, I don't think it's a good idea to tell Shanna, my-mom-as-a-twelve-year-old, that I'm visiting her from the future. Or she's visiting me from the past? Either way, I have a strong gut feeling that I should keep this knowledge to myself.

I take a deep breath and meet Shanna's eyes. "My grandparents," I say. "They live here, in Connecticut. And we're visiting from Maryland."

Shanna nods. "I've never been to Maryland."

Oh, you will someday, I almost say to her. *You'll live there and raise your family there. You'll make your daughter go to a special school there and play the violin there and—*

"It's a lot like here," I tell her. "But I live in a more suburban place."

She sighs. "I wish I lived in the suburbs! It's so boring here."

I laugh. "The suburbs are pretty boring too."

"But I bet you can walk to, like, a grocery store or something, right? A community pool in the summer? Anything?"

"Yeah, both those things, I guess."

"See?" Shanna says excitedly. "That's all I want! Here I can't walk to anything. The closest thing I can walk to is . . . well, this shed! And my neighbor's chicken coop. And some cows and horses. They're talking about building a library in town, but that's years away from being finished. Even during the school year I get bored. The bus drops me off in the afternoon and *whoosh*." She makes a yellow sound and a matching motion with her hand. "Nothing to do."

"But don't you, like, take after-school classes? Or play a sport? An instrument?" I've almost forgotten for a moment that this is, in some inexplicable way, my own mother as a girl. I've never thought to ask Mom what her childhood was like, but I assume she would've done tons of activities, considering how important it is to her that I'm constantly busy with the violin.

Shanna leans back, resting her weight on her hands behind her. "Nope. I wish. I'd give anything to do activities like that. Especially playing an instrument."

I feel a lump form in my throat as I put this together. I know from Mom's stories and photos that Grandma Florence and Grandpa Jack both worked full time and Mom was a "latchkey kid" in the nineties.

"My parents can't afford music lessons or anything," Shanna says. "Which is fine. I mean, who would even take me to lessons and stuff? They don't get home from work until six."

It's all adding up. I'm overwhelmed with emotions. I look Shanna in the eyes, searching for concrete proof that she's actually here and not a figment of my imagination. I want to reach out and touch her and find out if she's solid, whole—or just a wisp of a ghost.

I shiver. "I have to go," I tell her, standing up. I'm certain, at this moment, that whatever or whenever she is, she's at least real. And I can't just sit there anymore, making casual small talk with my sort-of-pre-mother person.

"Okay," she says, as if everything about this interaction is normal. "Maybe I'll see you back here. Tomorrow?"

I nod, though I have no idea if that's even possible. What is "tomorrow" for her, anyway? Is it the same as tomorrow for me? Are we on the same plane of the universe?

"Yes, for sure," I say in a confident kelly green, trying to hold it all together. "Tomorrow."

I open the door to abundant summer sunshine and the smell of freshly cut grass, scared to wonder what's just happened.

CHAPTER 3

a prima vista: literally "at first sight";
to sight-read a piece of music

Outside, everything looks the way it did before. My grandparents' house in the distance is the same sprawling collection of additions and extensions from various decades. So I'm definitely still in the present day. Maybe I can only time travel when I'm inside the shed. Or maybe the shed is outside of time somehow.

I watch the shed for a minute, but I don't see Shanna leave. Probably because she doesn't belong in this time. As I walk slowly back to the house, I wonder if she's now back in 1994 going about the rest of her day, or if she only exists inside the shed as some kind of echo or imprint or . . . whatever.

On the other hand, maybe I dreamed the entire

thing. Maybe I made it up. Maybe I heard that girl in a song and just thought I'd seen her with my eyes. It can be tricky in my brain sometimes—things I see can appear in my memories as sounds, and vice versa. But real or not, Shanna has sparked so many questions. Those questions swirl among the other fragments of music and color that are always intertwined with my thoughts.

All my life, my mother has seemed like a one-note melody to me—the person who gets the groceries, who drives me to music lessons, who tells me what to wear (things I'd never choose for myself) and when to practice (always). But there also must be some harmony to her. Something more complex happening beneath the surface.

If Shanna is my mother as a young girl, then *she* is the harmony. She's the complementary color, the other threads of music that fill out and deepen the melody. I can't imagine how the music of the girl in the shed fits with who Mom is today, but now I want to find out.

The long grass tickles my bare ankles, and the sun is starting to dip behind the big white house. I'm suddenly struck by the fear that I've ruined something—like by telling my-mom-as-a-twelve-year-old my name, I've somehow disrupted the space-time continuum and now she won't have named me Golden Rose because she's already met a girl named Golden Rose by the time I'm born?

My head throbs with the physics of it all. It's loud and gray and shiny in my brain, pounding to a time signature too fast to be used in any piece of music I could play.

Time. Time is linear. It's measured. It's a straight line. She cannot be my actual mother.

Then again, what about *Da Capo al Coda*? That's the musical instruction that tells you to replay a song from the beginning, until the coda, which takes the players on a different path from the first time. This could mean that time is actually . . . circular. Or at least meandering, somehow. Shanna in the shed is some kind of *Da Capo*—a starting point. But interacting with her might take me to a coda that changes everything.

The term *butterfly effect* pops into my head, a thick wisp of cotton, and I know I have to research this whole thing. I have to figure out how to not mess up in a time-travel situation.

I need the internet. Of course, I'm not allowed to use the internet, as punishment for my violin strike.

But if I tell Mom it's research, which isn't a lie, maybe she'll let me.

When I get to the house, I'm relieved just to see that she still actually exists. She's sitting in the glass sunroom with Grandpa Jack. Vienna barks at me as I squeak one of the double doors open, careful not to let her out, and Mom looks up. Grandpa Jack doesn't seem to hear anything. I guess his aids might not always work that well. Or maybe he turns their volume down when he doesn't feel like having a conversation. I sometimes wish I could turn the sound down in my head—that constant loop of music and thoughts and noise—so I get it.

"Rosie," Mom says, in a way that's both a greeting and a scolding. It's musical, but white and colorless. She *can't* be the girl from the shed. It makes no sense. And if she were, wouldn't she remember that she'd met me back when she was twelve? Maybe it was five minutes ago for me and thirty years ago for her, but she'd still remember it, right? Did I change our timeline or our history or our relationship by meeting her there? I search for clues in Mom's eyes, in her face, in her posture. But there's nothing.

"Mom . . ." I say, patting Vienna as if I'm not completely terrified by her, trying not to breathe in her smell or the scratchy texture of her fur. "I need to use your laptop, please. It's urgent. It's for a research project."

Mom raises her eyebrows. "Are you ready to start practicing the violin again?"

And I know now that what happened in the shed with Shanna hasn't had any ripple effects. Because that's the question Mom always asks lately, the same color red, the same intensity, with no nuance—no shadows of pink or highlights in yellow and orange. Nothing has changed with her.

I shake my head.

"Then no computer. No phone, no iPad, no internet. No tech until you play the violin again. And not just once—regular practice."

I shake my head again so she knows I mean it.

Mom sighs, a rainbow cacophony flowing out, so rich I can basically feel it. "You're lucky your grandparents still pay for cable," she mutters as she stands and heads toward the living room.

Grandpa Jack doesn't even look up. I don't think he's heard this entire conversation. He definitely doesn't hear in colors, that's for sure. I wonder, though, if he dreams in textures or words, or if he can see tastes or feel sounds. Someone in my family besides me must. I can't be the only one.

By the time I snap out of my thoughts, Mom is gone and Vienna has wandered over to her dog bed to curl up. Maybe *she* dreams in music or hears in textures. No one really knows how dogs think.

I've spent plenty of time on the internet looking up what's different about my brain. I know that most people don't see music or hear colors like I do. I know that what I have is called synesthesia and it's mostly harmless, according to the experts who don't have to deal with constant musical tracks playing in their heads or intense headaches from crowded areas. I also know that it's sometimes hereditary.

I've looked for clues in each of my parents—clues that they have synesthesia too—but I can't quite imagine either of them seeing color in the words and music of life, or hearing sounds when they look at something. In fact, that would probably be distracting and dangerous for Dad as a surgeon. And for Mom?

I've always assumed there wasn't much music in her, but thinking of Shanna—well, that changes everything. If that girl is somehow my mother, then there's more to Mom than I thought, more light and spark and harmony.

I watch Grandpa Jack in the sunlight that streams through the glass wall behind the couch. He's reading a newspaper, occasionally *harrumph*ing at whatever the news is. After hesitating for a second, I sit down in one of the chairs near him.

Neither of us speaks. I know he knows I'm there because his eyes flicked up ever so slightly when I came around the side of the couch.

At a loss for what to say or do, I look around the room. Against one wall is what Mom calls a "wet bar," which is some kind of grown-up drinks station that smells like the brown alcohol Dad likes to sip at night, slowly, with one ice cube melting into it. There's a TV in one corner that looks like it's from the 1980s.

Suddenly, inspiration strikes. "Grandpa Jack?" I say loudly, to make sure he hears. When I'm loud it's like a tree trunk—solid and brown, sturdy and buoyant and dense.

He peers at me over his glasses, which have slipped down his nose.

"Do you have any books about time travel?" I ask.

"Time what?"

I worry my bottom lip. "How about an encyclopedia? Or any, um, reference books?"

Grandpa Jack shifts in his seat to face me. "I think your mother donated most of our books to the library when she visited last summer."

The library!

"Thank you, Grandpa Jack! That's perfect!" The library is an absolutely brilliant idea. "Um, where *is* the library?" I ask, realizing I can't exactly google it.

"Down Hawthorne Road about half a mile—easy walk. On the right. Big white building. You can't miss it." And he goes back to his newspaper.

"Thank you!" I say again.

The library! Why didn't I think of that sooner? There must be computers there, and what my mother doesn't know can't hurt her! There'll probably also be a helpful book or two. I just need to know how to not mess anything up with Shanna. I'm not sure what I want to ask her or what I want to say, but I know I can't risk saying something that will cause me to not even be born in the future. As far as I can tell, I didn't change anything today, but that doesn't mean it's not possible. And I have to make sure that, if I do change something, it's in a good way.

Outside, the sky is alive with the colors of the sunset. Tchaikovsky's Violin Concerto in D major, op. 35, begins playing in my head when I see it, the spikes of orange arching above the tufts of purples and pinks.

I must've been in the shed longer than I realized. It's probably close to dinnertime now, so I'll have to wait until tomorrow morning to go to the library.

Of course, by then I might decide that I dreamed or imagined Shanna after all. But . . . I hope that's not the case. I want her to be real, and I want to see her again.

CHAPTER 4

music: sounds arranged in specific timing,
using the elements of melody, harmony,
rhythm, and timbre

I wake up at six, my internal violin-practicing-obsessed alarm as sharp as ever. I can smell something delicious. It has to be something Grandpa Jack is cooking, because the housekeeper, Tamar, doesn't fix breakfast, and nothing Mom has ever made has smelled that good.

Despite my eagerness to get to the library, my stomach rumbles and I know I won't be able to pass up the chance to eat whatever smells that amazing before I head out. I toss on my blue tank top and cutoff jean shorts—the ones that Mom hates but that make me think of Stravinsky's Violin Concerto from 1931, with all its rich shades of azure and turquoise. I don't brush my teeth or hair before heading downstairs.

The dining room table has been set for three. I can't imagine why—Mom hasn't had a real, sit-down morning meal in as long as I can remember. She usually makes a shake or a smoothie that she guzzles in the car on our way to school.

I've found the source of the enticing smell, though: a plate of bacon in the center of the table, next to a platter of pancakes. I recognize bacon from TV shows and movies, but my parents—despite being barely-practicing Jews—decided the one rule of Judaism they'd follow was no pork or shellfish, so I've never eaten it. I catalog the smell and the visual tucked together into my brain, along with a good association and the anticipation of actually tasting it.

I almost trip over Vienna, who's lying directly in the threshold of the door that separates the dining room from the kitchen. It's one of those old-fashioned doors that swings both ways, so you push it from either side depending on whether you want to enter or exit, both of which Vienna has made impossible.

"Move it, girl," I say, nudging her gently with my hands. Vienna is strong and quite heavy, and she doesn't budge for me. Only when Grandpa Jack comes near the door, whistling, does the dog move.

The clink of her tags jingling is a beautiful yellow run of scales, and Grandpa Jack's whistling adds the accompanying *arpeggios* in red.

"Good morning!" he says, as if he's been expecting me to join him for breakfast even though we never discussed it. "Get yourself some orange juice," he tells me, nodding toward the kitchen.

Now that Vienna has resettled in a patch of sun by the bay window overlooking the terrace, I can step into the kitchen. It's a mess of flour and dirty dishes, but I quickly find a glass in a cabinet and fill it with OJ from the fridge.

I walk back into the dining room, wondering too late if I should've gotten a glass of juice for Grandpa Jack too. I want to ask him if he wants anything, but it's his house and I feel suddenly awkward, like I don't belong at all.

"Sit, sit," he urges me, and I put down my OJ next to a place setting at one end of the table. "Did you sleep well?" he asks.

I nod, having just taken a sip of juice. When Grandpa Jack gestures to the plate of pancakes, I help myself to a few.

There's syrup and butter and everything, and the pancakes are still warm. He's timed his cooking perfectly.

"How did you know when I'd wake up?" I ask. Vienna stretches, craning her neck to cast me a skeptical glance. I'd be offended if I actually liked dogs. She seems about as disinterested in me as I am in her, which is only fair.

"Lucky guess." Grandpa Jack takes some bacon and motions for me to do the same.

I gingerly pick up one piece and, looking around to make sure Mom is nowhere in sight, take a bite. It melts on my tongue, and I suppress a hum of appreciation. It's the most delicious thing I've ever tasted.

Grandpa Jack seems different this morning, like he's more alert. We eat breakfast without talking, but it seems somehow friendlier than yesterday's silence—less motivated by him not being able to hear me and more just like we're old friends who are used to a routine. As if we're actually family, or something like that.

When I've had my fill of food, I look around, wondering where Mom is. Grandpa Jack has picked up today's newspaper and is reading. The only sound in the room is Vienna's soft snoring.

I clear my throat. "I guess I'm finished," I say, making sure I'm loud enough for him to hear me.

Grandpa Jack puts the paper down and looks at me. "You run along," he says. "I'll take this into the kitchen later."

I frown. Mom has taught me that it's rude to not clear one's own dishes, and even though I know Tamar will get here soon and clean the kitchen and load the dishwasher, I don't want to be the kind of person who just leaves a mess for her. I start to gather my plate and glass to carry to the kitchen, but Grandpa Jack scoffs.

"I'll do this. You go play."

"Okay," I say. "If . . . that's okay."

He doesn't take his eyes off the newspaper, but he smiles absently and nods.

I step over Vienna on my way out of the dining room. Before I go to the shed again, I want to do some research.

"May I go to the library?" I ask Mom when I find her. She's perched on the couch in the sunroom, looking at something on her laptop.

"How will you get there?" she asks without looking up from the screen.

"I'll walk. Grandpa Jack told me where it is."

Her eyebrow quirks slightly and her eyes drift over to me for a split second. "Fine. Have a good time. Be back home by five."

♪

Going to the library seems like the kind of thing normal kids do all the time, when they're not practicing the violin because they're not prodigies. Regular kids probably meet up at the library. They hang out there and . . . read together? Play video games on the computers there? Ugh, I'm awful at guessing what regular kids do. How am I supposed to figure it out without someone to teach me? I need a guide.

Shanna could've been a good guide, had she not turned out to actually be my mom thirty years ago. And possibly living only in my imagination or in that shed. Between the moments when I realized she wasn't a serial killer and when it became clear she was my mom as a kid, I had sort of hoped she was a totally normal girl who lived nearby and could teach me how to be normal.

But I'm not that kind of lucky. I'm born-with-an-unusual-brain lucky, and born-with-a-good-ear lucky, and I'm born-into-a-family-who-can-afford-a-ton-of-music-lessons lucky, if that last one even counts. But I've never been win-a-contest lucky or find-an-amazing-friend lucky.

It's hard to have friends when your life is the violin. Just ask Julianne.

Julianne used to be my best friend. I guess you could say she was my only friend. Until recently. And now I have no friends at all. I mean, I'm on good terms with Carlie and Kasey, two girls who also play violin in the Baltimore Children's Symphony. And there are some kids at school who are nice to me: Lorenzo, Kiki, Zahara, Paz. But I wouldn't say I'm actually close to any of them. Certainly not like I was with Julianne.

After we had our big fight, her mom even tried to call my mom to discuss it with her. Later that night, I heard my parents talking about it.

They assumed I was in my room and wouldn't overhear. Back then I was still obsessed with my music. If I wasn't playing, I was listening to recordings of maestros and principal violinists, live-streaming philharmonics, watching YouTube videos of everyone from Midori Goto to Isaac Stern.

But this particular night, I couldn't stop thinking about the fight with Julianne, and as soon as

Dad got home, Mom told him everything.

"Can you believe what that woman said to me?" Mom hissed. I could hear the clink of the china as she hand-washed her favorite dishes. She insists on using the fancy plates that aren't dishwasher safe, and Dad refuses to help wash them since we have perfectly good ones that can go in the dishwasher.

I heard Dad take the dinner leftovers and a beer out of the fridge before he even called upstairs to say hello to me—a greeting I ignored. I knew he'd assume I was working on music and wouldn't expect me to answer.

"She basically accused me of child abuse," Mom said. I could picture Dad, staring off into the middle distance, letting the sharp, dark purple ribbons of her voice unfurl around him.

I heard Dad put down his beer. "I'm sure she did not accuse you of child abuse."

Mom laughed, but it wasn't a happy laugh. "You weren't there, Pete. Trust me. She said that our kids could no longer be friends because she doesn't approve of our choices for Rosie."

"She said those words exactly?" Dad's words are almost always blue, but sometimes they turn gravelly navy or, like then, stormy gray-blue.

I heard a chair squeak across the floor as Mom

must've sat down next to Dad at the kitchen table. "She said Julianne is upset because Rosie is never available. She said that she can't handle Julianne's constant disappointment that Rosie can't go here or there because she has violin lessons, or a concert, or a fitting for an outfit for an upcoming performance. She said that Julianne needs some stability after her dad died, and I get it, but that woman essentially told me that if Rosie can't make more time for Julianne, she's going to find Julianne a new best friend. Can you believe that?"

My heart sank. I knew Julianne was sad sometimes because her dad had died. He'd had cancer for years, and the summer after fifth grade, he passed away. I'd missed the funeral because I was away at music camp in New York. Mom promised she'd go and give Julianne a hug for me. And she sent the family flowers, even though that's not something Jews do for funerals, because Julianne's family is Quaker and Buddhist. But how was *I* supposed to make Julianne feel better?

"What did you say?" Dad asked. Mom scoffed, like the sound of sour lemon juice, like the yellow color of your teeth feeling that juice erode them. I winced.

"I told her she should mind her own business. I told her she has no idea what it's like to have a child who is a literal prodigy like Rosie, someone who needs constant cultivation. I told her I'm sorry if her limp dishrag of a daughter is bored while Rosie is preparing for a career, but we cannot change our course just to make Julianne happy."

Dad laughed. "You did not say that."

"Not exactly," Mom allowed. "But I did try to explain how difficult it is to raise such a gifted child, one whose talents need all my attention. I can't just let Rosie play soccer or go to the pool like other kids. That would be a waste. It would be irresponsible. Rosie needs this, and it's a shame if Julianne is whiny about it at home, or feels 'left out' or whatever, but I cannot believe the nerve of that woman to actually *call me* and tell me how to raise my child!"

That was enough for me. I stepped back into my room from where I'd been perched in the hallway. I turned on Bach's Violin Concerto in A minor through the speakers that wirelessly attached to my iPad, and I flopped down onto my bed. I knew it'd be useless to text or email Julianne. We'd already said everything we could to each other, and now that I'd learned her mom was saying all the same things, I knew it would be impossible to make things right again. If they had ever been right at all.

The library smells like a symphony. Every imaginable word housed in the building's books mingles in my head to create something full and rich. It's not a song I recognize, but it's using every instrument.

The automatic doors whoosh purple, closing behind me, and I immediately see the children's section to my right. Tempting as it is to go there and get lost in a story, I instead turn left, where I see both a sign that reads *Reference* and a bank of computers. This is what Mom would call a "shortcut"—she thinks the internet is cheating in any context. But I know that the internet is going to be the quickest way to figure out what kind of magic or wormhole or accident has allowed my mother to exist both as her present-day self and as an apparition of her twelve-year-old self.

The computer area is completely empty—I have my pick of machines. I glance at the counter, where the reference librarian is reading. It seems like there's no fee or registration process to use the computers, so I choose one and sit.

The screens are all blank, which is my first clue that there's trouble. I hit the space bar, but the computer remains dark.

"Sorry—the internet's out," calls the librarian from her perch. She's not quiet, like I thought you were supposed to be in libraries. Her voice is orange and coarse but also friendly. She barely looks up from her book, though.

I let out a sigh and turn toward the reference shelves. Did Mom somehow come here and wipe out the internet just so I can't possibly have any tech access until I play the violin again? She says *I'm* stubborn but she's positively impossible, like a piece of string pulled so tight that nothing can get close without it snapping. If she can time travel back to being twelve, maybe she's also capable of controlling the public Wi-Fi.

The books lining the metal reference shelves look so old that they cannot possibly contain any current science. I mean, I assume that all the recent advances in technology and communication would have effects on time travel. These books seem like they were written before my mom was even born, so the likelihood of them containing information that would help me feels . . . small.

I'm prepared to head back to the children's section and look for a new historical fiction book to help me pass the time—being away from home plus not practicing the violin means tons and tons of extra time—when I see the top of a little staircase at the far side of the library. It's partially enclosed in plexiglass, so it must go down to the basement. There's a sign with an arrow that simply says *Theater.*

I'm intrigued, and the librarian is still absorbed in her book, so I decide to check out what's down there.

This isn't like me. At home, I do what I'm told—well, I did until I stopped practicing the violin. At school, I follow the rules. When I'm at violin lessons or the youth symphony, I'm focused on the music and would never dream of doing something that would distract me.

But this is my summer to be a regular kid. This is a random library in a town where I don't spend a lot of time. What are they going to do, ban me? Given the state of the reference section, I can't imagine that would be much of a loss.

I can hear a chorus of voices coming from the basement, a rainbow fluxing as several people speak at once. It sounds like a different language, but as I reach the gray concrete floor at the bottom of the steps, I realize it's a tongue twister.

"You know New York, you need New York, you know you need unique New York."

After repeating it a few times, one voice reigns chartreuse above the others. "Okay, everyone. Let's try it another way: *unique New York, you need New York*. Not starting with *you know New York*, okay? Take it again from the top."

And the rainbow chorus resumes, even more garbled this time as only a few voices seem to get it right according to the new instructions. I estimate from the sound that there are seven or eight people talking.

The voices are coming from a door to my left. Light spills out of a small window built into the door, and I peek inside. The window is partly covered by a poster—a schedule for the room. Between the 10 a.m. mommy-and-me class and several afternoon dance classes, I spot the listing for what's happening right now:

Monday/Wednesday/Friday
10:30 a.m.–12:00 p.m.
Hawthorne Parks and Rec
Summer Camp Class: Improv

Even with the poster covering most of the window, I can still see fully into the room. And conveniently, it makes my peering face less noticeable to anyone inside.

There's a circle of people—teenagers, a little older than I am—grinning and swaying as they recite the tongue twister. It's fairly clear who's leading the group: a woman who's maybe in her early twenties. She walks around the perimeter of the circle, nodding and encouraging the others with her hands. She reminds me of Dr. Sascha, the conductor of the Baltimore Children's Symphony back home, where I play—where I used to play.

Dr. Sascha is older than the teacher in charge here, but she's young for someone who's so accomplished. I don't know her exact age, but I can tell she's not as old as my mom, who's in her forties. Dr. Sascha has been conducting for so long because she was a child prodigy, like I am. She played the piano, studied at Juilliard when she was only fifteen, got her doctorate in performance at Peabody, and started conducting symphonies and philharmonics all over the world. She says I could do the same thing as a violin soloist. She wants me to go to Juilliard like she did, or maybe Peabody if I want to live at home.

I force those violin-related thoughts out of my mind and focus instead on the group of teenagers in this brightly lit room. Now they're sitting in a circle, playing some game where they point at each other and say nonsense words—"zip, zap, zop"—as fast as they can. There's a white boy using a wheelchair, a white girl dressed all in black, a dark-skinned kid who's super tall even sitting down, and a few others I can't see from this angle, maybe ten in all.

One boy keeps getting my attention. He's broad shouldered and has muscular arms, but his legs are skinny, folded beneath him. He has longish, straight, floppy hair that falls over one eye, and a crooked smile. He looks to be of Asian descent, with pale skin and dark hair, and he wears a polo shirt with a collar—like the ones Dad wears when he plays golf on the two or three weekends a year he isn't working and pretends to be one of those dads who can "relax" or just "hang out." (He is not one of those dads.)

"Mason," I hear another kid call the boy as I watch them all play the zip-zap-zop game. "Dude, stop making me laugh," the other kid tells him. I see how Mason's easy confidence and infectious smile could make someone laugh.

The girl sitting next to Mason is laughing too, and I can tell by the way she tosses her long, purple-streaked hair while she looks at him that she likes him. I hear someone call the girl Sunita as the kids stand up and move over to the wall, where the teacher—I hear someone refer to her as Mia—tells them to strike different poses.

Obviously, thanks to the poster, I know this is an improv class. And improv is kind of like theater, but without a script? I'm not totally sure. Julianne always wanted me to do something like this with her—take a class after school, like drama or art, something that had nothing to do with music. I told her I didn't have time. I literally didn't have one free day after school. And that was part of the big fight.

Mason leads the class in some kind of stretching exercise—kind of like yoga, but maybe more like dance. It's mesmerizing. Mostly because of Mason's self-assurance.

I spend time with a lot of confident people, especially confident boys. Violinists have a reputation for being full of themselves. But Mason isn't arrogant. He just seems comfortable. Assured. Happy in his own skin. Gosh, I want to know what that feels like.

Eventually Mia says, "Good work today, everyone! Tomorrow we're going to talk about your showcase and break you up into groups for skits."

I realize they're all starting to gather their things

and head toward the door, so I retreat, ducking into the intersecting hallway around the corner.

Mason emerges first, followed by Sunita. In cool tones of green and turquoise, she's telling him that she has soccer later but plans to be at the pool after five.

Mason doesn't seem all that interested, as he's focused on pushing the elevator button so that the kid with the wheelchair—Ryan, white skin with red hair—can glide in as the doors open.

"Coming with?" Ryan asks Mason, and Mason follows him, waving to Sunita as the doors close.

Sunita waits for the girl dressed all in black, and they climb the stairs together, gesturing wildly, laughing and whispering. Like friends.

No one has noticed me, which doesn't surprise me. I've always been the girl who is invisible, unless I'm onstage with my violin.

CHAPTER 5

tempo: the speed at which music is played;
time

When I get back to my grandparents' house, the
only logical thing to do is to head straight to the
shed. I have to know if I made the whole thing up,
or if I'm losing my mind, or if there is such a thing
as time travel, or if someone's playing a prank on me.
It doesn't even matter that I didn't manage to do any
research at the library. I can investigate on my own.
If I don't see the girl again, I'll know she was a fluke,
a figment of my imagination. If I do see her, I can
gather more clues about her, about what's going on.
Whether she's a ghost or an actor or a figment of my
imagination, I have questions for her.

As I approach the shed, I look for evidence that
it's magical or haunted. It seems like a completely

average shed, humming the dull brown of aged wood that I barely register in my ears because it's such a common color. It's the same dull brown of tree trunks and city buildings and dirt roads and bland food. It's a background melody I can tune out. The shed doesn't have windows, and I try to remember how there was light in there the other day. I don't think there was any electricity, but as I circle the shed, noticing the cinder blocks lifting one side of it where it rests on the slight downhill slope, I confirm that there is no window.

The door handle is dusty, with no sign of fingerprints from the previous day.

The door creaks its silver *glissando* again as I push it open, and I let my eyes adjust. It's not completely dark inside. A shaft of light showcases the dust in the air, and I realize, with a smile, that there's a skylight. That's how I can see in here. I'm staring up at it when I hear her voice on a cloud of pink breeze.

"Oh, hi," says Shanna. I take her in more fully than I was able to the first time we met. Her frizzy curls are pulled into a ponytail on the top of her head, and I can see her face more clearly. Shanna's chin is pointy and her cheekbones sharp; her eyes are velvety brown, and today she has sunglasses on top of her head, like she's a movie star or something. Of course, what I notice most are her colors—magentas and golds and bright grassy greens. She's an up-tempo song with sad notes slipped in. She's bursting with sound even when she is still.

"Hi," I say softly, remembering all at once that Shanna is—was? might be, someday?—my mother. Before she was my mother.

"I'm hiding," Shanna whispers. It takes me by surprise, the cool silver of her breath.

I look around, suddenly nervous. "Hiding from who?" My heart pounds as I worry that this dream or apparition is not just bizarre, but also somehow dangerous.

"From what," she corrects me. It takes me a moment to process what she's getting at.

I roll my eyes impatiently. "Okay, *what* are you hiding from?"

"My dog," she whispers. This time her whisper is purple with joy.

I'm so relieved that I let out a laugh. Its green mixes with her purple whisper in the air between us and I feel calm again. It's as if a spell has been cast, and I don't have the energy or willpower to worry about the logistics of Shanna and the shed at the moment. I'm just happy that whatever-this-is is still here, still working.

"I'm training my new puppy," she says proudly. "I'm trying to teach him to be in a crate when I leave the house. I mean, to *enjoy* being in the crate. I can put him in there no problem, but the part where he learns to like it is a different story."

I nod, though I have no idea what Shanna is talking about. I just like watching her. I like seeing her happy as she talks about her puppy.

I sit cross-legged on the floor, right in the pocket of sun from the skylight, not caring that the floor's dusty. Shanna joins me. There's just enough space for both of us in the square of sunshine. "So you're hiding in here?" I prompt, just wanting to hear her say more.

Shanna leans back on her hands, her face partially in the light and partially shaded. "I can't stand hearing him cry while he gets used to the crate!"

I nod as if I understand. I can imagine how painful that would be to listen to—the angry reds and the forlorn blackness of the cries.

"We got him a few weeks ago. I've been begging for the longest time to get a puppy. And my parents finally said yes. Of course, I have to do all the work—I have to walk him and train him and feed him, but I don't even mind! I *want* to do all that. I love dogs. And my puppy is the sweetest."

I stop myself before I ask to see a picture, remembering that, if Shanna is somehow actually my mom in the 1990s, she wouldn't have a cell phone with a photo of the dog. Instead I ask, "What's his name?"

Her face lights up, and I can hear the way the light glints brightly off her face. "Stimpy!" she tells me.

The spell is broken. I feel nauseated. I remember that name.

"Stimpy?" I repeat, as if there's any chance this isn't the dog I've heard about.

Shanna nods. "Like the cartoon *Ren and Stimpy*."

Oh no. What do I do?

I try to think fast. I don't know the rules of time travel, but if this is anything like the time-bending stories I've read and seen, I have to be really careful with the space-time continuum. If I say something that changes what happens to Stimpy, could it set off a whole new chain of events that would somehow mean that my mother never meets my father and I'm never born?

No, there's no way something this small could lead to a huge change like that. And I can't stand by and say nothing, not when I know what I know about Stimpy.

Besides, whispers a little voice in a corner of my brain, a simple quiet melody playing on a brand-new channel in there, *what if it changes something for the better?* What if I save Stimpy, and then my mom keeps loving dogs? What other small things could I change with this power? Can I say something tiny but clever that will make her chill out about me playing the violin?

My mind's racing. I grab at the first idea that materializes. "Do you have a leash?"

Shanna gives me a quizzical look I recognize; it's a look I see on Mom's face every day. On Shanna, there are fewer wrinkles and lines, but it's the same scrunched nose and *are you serious?* vibe. It radiates orange and makes my ears hurt. "Of course I have a leash."

I bite the inside of my cheek. This is not as easy as I hoped it would be. "That's good," I say. "I know it sounds, like, really simple, but . . . just please keep the dog on the leash all the time."

Shanna's quizzical look morphs into the exasperated one I also recognize from Mom's face. I've seen this one *a lot* since I started the violin strike. "Oooookay."

"I just . . ." I search for a way to warn her without giving away what I know happened—or will happen—to Stimpy. I can't say it. Like, literally, I'm not sure it's possible. There are limits, I sense, to what I'm allowed to say here. Certain sounds won't reverberate in the shed. Certain words won't cross time and space.

"Please just be really careful," I tell her.

Shanna laughs. "I'm a very responsible person," she says. And with that, she stands up. "I should get going."

"Yeah, me too. I'll see you later." I jump up and head out the door, eager to escape the stress of this conversation.

I hope I haven't said too much—not enough to ruin the space-time continuum and make it so that I was never born, but just enough to change one tiny thing. For now.

I was probably around four years old when I realized I could listen to any song or piece of music over and over again in my head. It's like Spotify in my brain; once I've heard it, I can hear it again any time

I want. Maybe I could always do this, but I was four when I registered that it was something most other people *couldn't* do. I had stopped taking naps, and Mom, who was still trying to work part-time from home back then, was exasperated with me. She told me to go sit in my room and be quiet.

"How am I supposed to even have a moment to breathe?" I heard her mutter.

Even whispered, I could tell her words were blue and gray, sad and trapped and desperate.

"It's okay, Mama," I told her. "I'll just go listen to some music."

I sat down on the edge of my bed—it was really my crib with one side taken off so I could get myself in and out—and closed my eyes. I'd heard a song on Mom's car radio the day before, on the classical station she played whenever she took me to go grocery shopping. It was a piano song that had the same blues and grays I heard in Mom's voice when she said she wanted a moment to breathe, so I played it in my mind over and over, until I could fully see all the layers of color in the piece.

Next, I played Dad's favorite song. I'd heard it a thousand times but could never get over the weight and beauty of the heights and depths the notes scaled.

It was one of the unusual songs that contained every shade of the rainbow.

By the time Mom came in to get me, it had probably been an hour. I'd made it through several other classical pieces I knew, as well as a few pop songs and Broadway hits my parents played in the evenings after dinner.

"I thought you were going to listen to music," Mom said.

I stretched and climbed out of bed. "I did."

She looked around my room, confused. At that time, there were shelves filled with books I couldn't yet read and stuffed animals I rarely played with, but there was no way to play music. I didn't have a computer or an iPad, or even an old record player like the one Dad treasured and told me to never, ever touch.

"Don't lie to me," Mom said, exasperated. Her words had morphed from blues and grays into the mean, tired green of frustration.

Tears filled my eyes. "But I did. I played music in my mind."

"What?" The green buzz of her frustration got so loud, I had to close my eyes.

"'*Lent et douloureux*,'" I said, pronouncing the

73

French perfectly since I'd heard the man on the classical radio station say it that way the day before. "And then 'Air on the G String,' and the *Brandenburg Concertos,* and . . ."

I trailed off when I saw how stricken she looked. She already knew I picked up music easily and had gotten me my own tiny violin for lessons, but this was something new. She studied me, unblinking. "Rosie, that's not . . . it's not normal."

I blinked at her. I'd assumed that everyone listened to music in their heads sometimes.

Mom knelt down so that we were eye to eye. "It's—it's okay, honey. You can still do it. Just don't tell anyone else, okay?"

I remember the feel of my bed's comforter beneath my hands as I braced myself, leaning away from her darkening whispers, which had gone from frustration green to the dark greens of a forest's understory. "I thought we liked music."

"We do! And it's great for you to play music, to stand out when you're performing or practicing. But some things . . . some things other people can't understand, so we don't share them."

That's how I knew I could never tell my mother about how I could see colors when I heard sounds.

I knew that if she didn't want anyone to know I could play symphonies in my head, she would definitely not want me announcing to the world that the color of a perfect middle C is yellow, or that sometimes whispers are blue but they can also be pink depending on the meaning of the words. I couldn't tell her that a painting could be a symphony, that a song can be a picture. I knew, instinctively, that she would see it as something bad, something wrong in my brain. Something I had to hide.

Back at the house, everything seems pretty much the same as it was yesterday afternoon. Vienna is blocking the logical entrance behind the French doors, forcing me to leap over her. Grandpa Jack is in the sunroom reading a newspaper. Tamar is in the kitchen doing dishes. The only difference is that Mom is nowhere to be seen.

It's just as well.

"Hi, Grandpa Jack," I say, flopping down in the chair across from his spot on the couch.

He looks up briefly. "You don't need to call me *Grandpa* Jack," he says. "It's redundant." So he's asking me to just call him Jack? That seems kind of . . . distant.

I guess this is his way of telling me not to expect anything from him. Like he's saying, *Let's let this "Grandpa" nonsense go, shall we? We're just two humans who happen to be in the same house for a few weeks.* And I get it. We've never had much of a relationship.

"Rosie is too busy with rehearsals to come visit you," I've heard Mom say on the phone.

Or "I can't just leave Rosie and drive up there— she has a concert!"

My favorite excuse is this one: "Who else will supervise Rosie's violin practice at home?" which is hilarious because I've been practicing on my own since I was seven.

But Mom has her reasons, I guess. She calls her parents exactly once a week. They never video chat, just talk on the phone. She usually does it while she's walking on the treadmill in the basement, so as not to "waste time." She's pretty big on not wasting time.

Mom is happiest when she's in motion. I rarely see her sit down and rest. She has no favorite TV shows or books, but I guess I'm not one to talk, as I don't either.

Julianne is always talking about this sci-fi/fantasy book series, The Garden of Fairy, and I almost feel as though I've read the first two or three volumes because I used to listen to her talk about them so much. Last I heard from Julianne, back when we still ate lunch together at school, there was going to be a TV series based on the books, which means she'll be even more obsessed when it starts airing in the fall and will probably recap episodes at lunch.

Not that I'll be sitting with her, of course. She'll be with Amelia and Isabela, I guess, and I'll be at the end of a long table with some kids who don't have strong feelings about lunch seating arrangements. Which is fine. I don't really like to talk through lunch. I've never been good at multitasking. I was happy to just listen to Julianne—happier when it was about something other than The Garden of Fairy, but whatever.

The carpet covering most of my grandparents' floors muffles the sound of Mom's footsteps approaching behind me, and I'm instead startled by her very bright yellow-green, very cheerful voice interrupting my thoughts.

"How was your outing?"

"Fine," I say, casually violet, without even thinking. I don't look up at her, but once she's sitting down on the chair across from Grandpa Jack, I study her.

I look for clues that she is Shanna, and vice versa.

She's tapping away on her iPad, probably arranging things for Grandma Florence or texting Dad or . . . whatever it is she usually does all day when I'm at school, which, I honestly don't know.

I stare at my mother, her shadows long and deep in the part of the sunroom where the shelves block the light. And suddenly, I miss her. She's here, but also, I *miss* her.

How can you love someone so much and also feel so angry at them? How can someone be right there, reading the news or placing a grocery delivery order, or chopping up lettuce for salad, and yet also be so many millions of miles away?

I think of how she's losing her own mother right now. *What will I do when you die?* I wonder. And *How can I ever exist without you?*

Yet at the same time, I'm so mad. That she can't see me. That she can't hear me. That she wants me to be a little music box, performing at her whim, perfect and orderly and predictable.

It's like there's a thunderstorm in my brain—the hot and the cold, the light and the dark, the warring extremes of those contrasting emotions, ending up in shades of silver and gray, flashes of light so bright they hurt my ears.

As if she can feel me watching her, Mom looks right at me. "Rosie, go keep your grandmother company for a little while, would you?"

I look around, as if Grandpa Jack or Vienna might offer some excuse, some escape for me.

Vienna keeps sleeping and Grandpa Jack doesn't seem to hear a thing. I can't think of a reason not to go upstairs, aside from the fact that I'm terrified of death—of the gray sounds of pain and labored breathing, of Grandma Florence's confusion and frailty. I know it's not contagious, and yet . . . some-day I, like Grandma Florence, will reach the end of my time on Earth. Maybe in the dramatic finish of a symphony like Sibelius's Symphony no. 2, or maybe in a quiet fading out of sound, a blue becoming paler and paler until it's white.

At the top of the stairs, I pause at the door to the main bedroom, praying that Grandma Florence is asleep so I can return downstairs and tell Mom that I tried. But as soon as I peek my head around the doorframe, Grandma Florence's eyes dart over to me.

"Hi," I say. My voice sounds small and pink, yet it echoes in the large, darkened room. The hum of a humidifier running in the corner clashes with the pink of my voice, the notes dissonant and unpleasant together.

I step inside, and Grandma Florence seems to perk up ever so slightly. "Rosie?"

I nod, shocked again that she somehow recognizes me, bracing for what will follow.

"Did you bring your violin?" she asks, looking behind me, as if I might be hiding it.

I stop just a few feet into the room, staring down at the warm, light brown wood of the floors. "No, I'm sorry, I didn't."

Grandma Florence closes her eyes and lets her head rest on the pillow behind her. "Please play the violin for me?" she asks.

I shake my head even though she can't see me. "I'm sorry, but I can't," I tell her softly, in tones that harmonize with the sound of her breathing, doing the best I can to be soothing.

Time ticks by, the steady eighth notes of the air conditioning and the humidifier mixed with Grandma Florence's half-note breaths. By the time I realize she's asleep, my own breaths have synchronized with hers, and when I close the bedroom door behind me, I imagine it's the soft, final drumbeat of a song I haven't yet learned.

CHAPTER 6

staccato: musical notes that are
brief and detached

By Monday, my fifth day here, breakfast is becoming this quiet routine that Grandpa Jack and I do together. He makes the bacon and the pancakes or eggs; I put bread in the toaster. He's made coffee long before I wake, and I pour orange juice for myself.

We mostly eat in silence—well, *we're* silent. Vienna makes noises that I would've thought were gross just a few days ago, but I've gotten used to her slobbery gray chortles. And it's nice that the house has some sounds of life in it. Mom is still asleep. Tamar will be here soon, and the visiting nurse is already upstairs with Grandma Florence, but there's a stillness to the place, as if it's holding its breath, waiting for something. Or someone.

That makes me think of Shanna.

"Grandpa Jack?" The words take over for my brain, tumbling out like a yellow ribbon I didn't know would unfurl. "Do you believe in time travel?"

"I thought we were dropping the 'Grandpa,'" he says, and I wonder if he even heard my question. I'm slightly relieved and imagine coiling up the yellow ribbon I let go.

Suddenly an idea strikes me, a compromise. "How about we drop the 'Jack' instead?" I ask, with a boldness I didn't know I had, something deep like purple and coffee and thunder. For some reason, I can't just call him Jack. I can't. I'm finally visiting for more than just a day or two—I finally have a chance to actually know him. I don't want him to forget what we are to each other before we even begin.

He makes a somewhat-affirmative *harrumph*, and I smile.

"Time travel, you say?" he asks.

"Oh." I had been okay with him having not heard me, but it seems like he did. "Never mind. It's silly. I know no one—"

"Of course I believe in time travel."

We stare at each other, his words a dull silver string between us.

"You do?" I whisper.

He barely moves, but I see his left eyebrow quirk the tiniest bit.

Maybe the magic has permeated the house. Maybe the magic is genetic. Maybe time travel runs in our family. Maybe—

"I'll show you," Grandpa says.

I watch as he rises and crosses to the living room, to the shelves that hold stacks and stacks of photo albums. The kind of photos you used to take with a camera on film, as Mom likes to remind me. She wants me to be as careful taking pictures with her phone as I'd be "if each one were on film—film that costs money." And this is why I always tell her I need my own phone, which has become one of our favorite arguments. Or at least it was until I went on my violin strike.

Grandpa returns to the table with a photo album. I hold my breath, waiting to find out the secret of Shanna and the shed and Grandpa and me.

"This is from 1972," he says. "The year I married your grandmother." The pictures are in sepia tones—reds and pinks and browns, like his words, full of love and something that feels a little like sadness. Regret, maybe?

I peer at a photo of Grandma Florence, her white wedding dress train spread out all around her.

"Beautiful," I say. "I can practically smell the roses she's carrying." I don't tell him that I'm practically hearing a symphony because of the picture.

Grandpa nods. "See? Time travel." He leans back on his chair, stretching out his legs.

I shake my head. "What do you mean?"

"You're in the dining room, right now, with me." Grandpa taps the photo with his finger, curved from arthritis and time, his nail brittle and short. "But you're also here. In Congregation Isaiah, in 1972. Smelling the roses."

Disappointment rushes out of me with my breath. It was a false alarm, a red herring. A harsh red, not like the pinks and browns of the sepia photos.

"I see what you mean," I say quietly. "Thanks for showing me."

Before the tears can spill out over my eyelashes and onto my cheeks, I clear my plate and head back into the kitchen.

"Rosie," he calls after me.

I take in a breath and turn to him.

Something is different in Grandpa's gaze now, as if he senses that his version of time travel wasn't what I was looking for. "What are you doing with your day?"

I shrug. "I'm going to the library again, but . . ." I do some calculations in my head. It's only seven thirty in the morning and I want to time my visit there just right to see that improv class. ". . . not until later."

Grandpa smiles. "Do you know how to swim?"

I like swimming enough. I used to go to our local community pool with Julianne in the summers, maybe once or twice a week, when I had the time. We'd spend most of our hours there deciding where to sit, then artfully arranging our towels over the slatted plastic chairs and looking around to see who else from our school was there. Sometimes Julianne would try to flirt with this lifeguard she had a crush on, which I never understood. I mean, the lifeguard was pretty, but she was probably at least seventeen, and there's no way she was going to have any interest in a middle schooler, so what was even the point?

I know how to swim from lessons I took when I was little, before my days became consumed with music camp and rehearsals. I have enough skill that I'm not worried about drowning or anything, but I also don't want to be in a position where I actually *need* to swim, for real, for any significant distance. I don't think I've swum in Grandpa and Grandma's pool since I was eight or nine.

Still, I put on my plain blue suit and a pair of yellow cotton shorts over them, find my flip-flops at the bottom of my still-not-completely unpacked suitcase, and go downstairs to meet Grandpa Jack. He's already by the sunroom door, with a canvas bag slung over his shoulder, petting Vienna and staring off into the distance.

I hesitate, feeling shy, not wanting to disrupt the silence. I can see one side of Grandpa Jack's face as he takes in the green expanse of the fields. The coat of mist over the grass is burning off, but a little bit still lingers. He smiles, as if remembering something that happened out there, replaying it in his mind, the way I can basically play the violin part of *Salut d'Amour,* op. 12 in my sleep.

I hear the piece now, as I watch Grandpa Jack's face, and it makes me feel so sad. Sometimes the music feels bright and yellow, uplifting with promise, but this time, as I let it score his memory, I allow it to be blue. A sweet, melancholy blue that was once joyful but is now tinged with loss. I wonder what he's remembering. Time traveling in his mind.

Before the final lingering D sharp that trails off at the end of Opus 12—the one I've been told I use too much vibrato on but can't seem to stop playing with as much drama as possible—Grandpa Jack seems to shift back into the present and notices me watching him.

"Hi," I say shyly, the music stopping abruptly in my mind. After a moment of silent eye contact with Grandpa Jack, my brain shuffles and starts playing a different Edward Elgar piece in the background.

"Well, hello there," he says. "Shall we?" It's like he's welcoming me to a fancy ball.

"Um, towels?" I say as Grandpa Jack opens the door for me with one hand and holds Vienna in place with the other.

"Got one for you in the bag. And some goggles too."

He follows me out onto the terrace and closes the door, keeping Vienna safely inside. There's a little latch that prevents her from nudging the door open with her nose, and Grandpa secures it for good measure.

We use the stone steps to exit the terrace, instead of jumping off the ledge the way I like to do. That's just as well, since I don't think Grandpa Jack should—or could—leap off the terrace. We walk toward the trees, in the opposite direction from the shed. The grass is still a little damp with dew, and there's a slight chill in the air.

"Do you swim often?" I ask to fill the silence.

"Most mornings," he says. "We've got a guy who comes once a week to maintain it, so it's like having my own personal YMCA."

He seems a little softer to me today, maybe a little happier. And suddenly I feel guilty, remembering that his wife is dying upstairs in the house and he has every reason to be gruff sometimes. How do I regularly forget that? Several questions spring to my mind, light gray with curiosity, but I push them all away. This isn't the time to ask him anything.

We head toward a break in the wall of green trees. There's a narrow, rickety bridge that spans a little creek. I cross the bridge behind Grandpa Jack, watching the dappled light make patterns on the back of his white shirt. The bridge has some newer-looking wooden slats and some that are much older, worn and weathered but not decaying.

On the far side of the bridge is a set of steep stone steps that ends in the flat pool area. The rectangular pool is surrounded by flowering azalea bushes and forsythia and tons of other plants whose names I don't know. There are so many of them that I almost can't see the narrow gravel driveway beyond them, running along the back edge of the property. Like paintings, the colors serenade me with their vibrant notes.

It's so much more beautiful than I remember.

"I hope you know it's not heated," Grandpa Jack grumbles as he descends the steps.

"That's fine," I say to his back. At the bottom of the steps, he puts his towel on a white lounge chair, so I do the same. Before I've even slid out of my flip-flops, Grandpa has peeled off his T-shirt, put on goggles, and walked into the pool.

As the water hits his bare belly, Grandpa exhales sharply, sounding more like Vienna than himself, and exclaims, "Mother Hubbard!"

The way he says it makes me laugh before I even fully process it. It's rare for me to make a sound without considering it first.

Grandpa ducks under the water and resurfaces, the droplets cascading down from the little hair he has left onto his shoulders, and I'm still laughing.

"What?" he asks, looking behind him.

I suddenly feel bad, not wanting Grandpa to think I'm laughing *at* him. I shake my head and gesture *no* with my hands. "Mother Hubbard . . ." I say through the gradual *rallentando* of my laughter.

Grandpa smiles. "It's better than the alternative."

I imagine him with Mom, when she was a girl, using this phrase instead of cursing. Now that I've "met" Shanna—or whatever you could call our interactions in the shed—I can so vividly picture her wearing a bathing suit similar to mine, preparing to join Grandpa Jack for a swim.

Time travel.

I walk to the edge of the pool and dip my toes into the water—which I immediately realize is a mistake, because it's *cold*!

"You have to just jump," Grandpa says, a faint smile on his lips. "You'll never do it if you just slowly put your feet in."

I know what he means. Like the shocking *fortissimo* chord in the second movement of Haydn's "Surprise Symphony," I jump into the deep end.

The water's still cold, but I wasn't expecting it to feel so refreshing. I sink with the force of my body hitting the water and allow myself to slowly rise to the top, floating on my back as soon as I do.

"Mother Hubbard," I say quietly, smiling up at the perfectly blue sky.

With graceful swim strokes, Grandpa's making his way from the deep end to the shallow end of the pool. I tread water for a minute so that I can watch him carry his body from one place to another, moving through the water like my bow gliding across the strings of my violin.

Every four strokes, like perfect quarter notes, he lifts his head to the side to breathe. Measure by measure, he swims in rhythm—somewhere between *adagio*, which is seventy to eighty beats per minute, and *andante*, more of a walking pace of seventy-six to a hundred and eight beats per minute.

Watching the gentle cadence of Grandpa swimming laps makes me want to try it too. I leave him plenty of room, positioning myself along the opposite side of the pool. My strokes aren't nearly as elegant or as smooth as Grandpa's, but I manage to move my body from one end of the pool and back. And again. And again.

At one point, I look over to Grandpa and our eyes meet while he raises his head to breathe. He gives me the slightest of smiles and a nod so I know he sees I'm swimming with him, parallel.

I swim along to Brahms's Violin Concerto in D Major, op. 77, the Itzhak Perlman version. I'm starting the third movement when I realize how tired my arms and shoulders are, and I see with relief that Grandpa is getting out of the pool.

"I didn't know you swam laps," he calls as I make my way to the steps. My armpits and back ache with the strains of unused muscles, but I'm grinning.

"Neither did I," I say brightly. "Until today."

Grandpa tosses me a towel and I cradle my face in it, feeling the warmth of my breaths, my heart pounding *vivace*, lively and fast.

We don't talk as we walk back up the grassy expanse toward the house. I can't find words to thank Grandpa for bringing me swimming with him. When we reach the doors to the sunroom, he turns and looks at me.

"Same time tomorrow?"

I nod, the smile curving onto my lips again.

I have just enough time to shower and change before I need to head to the library. Once I'm dressed, I dash into the kitchen to make myself a sandwich to bring on the walk to town. All the swimming has made me ravenous.

"Why is your hair wet?" asks Mom. She's behind me, startling me. I drop the knife I was holding and it clatters, a perfect B flat, onto the porcelain plate where my sandwich is almost complete.

"Hey, Mom," I say, turning. "I just took a shower. I went swimming with Grandpa earlier."

"How many times have I told you it's not safe to swim without an adult watching?" She sounds distracted, dismissive. Her azure tone vibrates against my skin, making my whole body bristle.

I cut my sandwich and wrap half of it in parchment paper I found in a drawer. "I just said I was with Grandpa," I mutter, taking a bite of the unwrapped half.

Mom reaches over me and grabs a slice of tomato from the platter of sandwich ingredients Tamar left for our lunch.

"I suppose he'll do," she says, slipping the tomato into her mouth and pressing her fingers to her lips as if to keep the juice in.

"What do you mean, 'he'll do'?" I take another bite of my sandwich, tasting the turkey and cheese and lettuce, each like separate instruments blending into song with the bread.

She turns back toward the swinging door that divides the kitchen from the dining room. "As a supervising adult," she says.

I roll my eyes at her back and call after her, "I'm going to the library."

"Home by five," she says, not even looking back.

It's strange, because just a few months ago—until I went on strike seventy-two days ago, to be exact—Mom had to know where I was and what I was doing at every moment. She had an opinion about my every move too. Going to the bathroom? Maybe I drank too much water. Feeling tired? I should get more sleep. Frustrated by a tricky section in a new sonata? Try that meditation app for three minutes and go back to it.

I'm suspicious of this new casualness, because Mom is like a general. She has tactical moves planned for every situation, and I'm suddenly sure that her seeming nonchalance about what I do with my time is some kind of bargaining chip I'm going to pay for later. It's some dangling carrot of freedom I'll have to exchange for something she wants—something violin-related, for certain—when I least expect it.

As I set off toward the library, I can't help thinking of Shanna. Of how the bright-eyed girl excited about her puppy became the woman who dislikes Vienna. Of how the girl who asks so many questions became the woman who has all the answers. Did it happen in this house? While she watched the sky from the sunroom windows, sat on the terrace, swung her legs against the rough gray stones stacked above the grass?

Maybe she was living out some melody that still echoes in her current self—another movement within the same symphony. She couldn't have become a *completely* different person over time. Could she? I shudder at that idea. I don't want to become someone else over time.

But if I continue to avoid playing the violin . . .

Maybe I've already become someone else.

In addition to being the conductor of the Baltimore Children's Symphony, Dr. Sascha is one of my official mentors. I have three—set up by Mom, naturally.

Aside from Dr. Sascha, there's Agnieszka, my violin technique teacher. She's in her sixties, probably, and we never talk about anything other than the violin when I go to her studio twice a week. I know she has grandchildren, though, because their photos line her cluttered piano.

Once a week I see Nikko for music theory, in a studio in the same building as Agnieszka's. Nikko is in his late twenties, I would guess, because he still talks about college and grad school like they were really recent, and he says that he and his husband talk about having kids all the time but think they're too young . . .

Saw. I *saw* Nikko for music theory, and I studi*ed* with Agnieszka twice a week. I haven't done either of those things in over two months now, not since I went on strike. When I told Nikko, he said it was cool and he'd still be around when I was ready to come back. Agnieszka scowled, but she's always scowling, and Mom told her we were just "taking a summer break to travel" and that we'd resume lessons in the fall. We'll see about that.

The person I felt really awful about disappointing, though, was Dr. Sascha. She's my favorite violin-related adult, because she treats me like a person and not just a brain and arms attached to a violin. And I can't stop thinking of her now, as I stand in the basement of the library, peeking through the window in the theater room's door, watching Mia the improv teacher talk to the class.

It's eleven o'clock, so the class is in full swing. Already I recognize some of the kids I watched the other day: Ryan with red hair and pale skin, Sunita with her purple-streaked ponytail, and Mason with the hair that flip-flops and makes my heart do the same.

Mia makes me think of Dr. Sascha, partly because they look alike. They're both short, blond, and fat—a word Dr. Sascha constantly says is "just an adjective like any other." But it's more than their physical similarities. Mia has the same sparkle in her eyes that Dr. Sascha has: a little mischief, a little kindness, a lot of enthusiasm. Mia looks like she could be Dr. Sascha's younger sibling, and I realize that I don't know if Dr. Sascha has any siblings, or any family at all. I've never asked her.

"In improv, we adopt the rule of 'yes, and,'" Mia says. She's walking around in a circle as she talks, and everyone in the class is paying rapt attention. "This leaves room for maximum creativity, brainstorming, and flexibility. Everything you say or do is fact, and then it's your partner's job to build onto whatever you've just established."

I'm wracking my brain to think of an equivalent of this concept in classical music. Nothing pops up right away. Cadenzas in solo concertos, maybe, but that only works with one person improvising at a time. A cadenza is like choosing a color palette, and that becomes the rule. You can play all sorts of notes in shades of blue, for example, but you have to avoid oranges, which clash, or yellows or reds, which would completely change the blues into greens or purples.

I watch the rest of the class session, the rigid notes of Bach and Beethoven reverberating in the neverending radio that lives inside my head, trying to reconcile this "yes, and" idea of with the kind of music I've devoted my entire life to. The kind of notes that exist permanently, in black and white on a page. The notes that haven't changed in hundreds of years.

Despite the vibrant colors I constantly see and the cascade of musical notes I can't quiet inside my unusual brain, I've been very much like these black-and-white pages all my life. Until I went on strike. I didn't exactly say "yes, and" when I stopped playing. I think I said, "No, but." Still, maybe that's something. Maybe it's a beginning.

I check the schedule on the door and make sure I leave a couple of minutes before the class is supposed to end. Nothing would ruin my delight in observing Mia and her class like getting caught.

CHAPTER 7

pianissimo: very gently, softer than *piano*

Before I leave the library, where the internet is back up and running, I spend a little time on one of the computers, searching for helpful information about time travel. There's nothing that really comes close to my situation—at least nothing that seems legitimate and not sketchy. Eventually I settle for checking out a few books with time-bending elements in them.

But once I'm back at my grandparents' house and have a chance to read through the books, they turn out to be pretty useless too. I don't find any clues as to why and how one might encounter one's mother in a shed as her twelve-year-old self, or any instructions for what to say and do to ensure that one doesn't disrupt the space-time continuum.

Without a roadmap for how to deal with this

situation, I'm dreading returning to the shed. If Stimpy meets the fate I expect, it'll be so sad—and it'll prove I can't change anything about the past for the better. If something different happens, that'll mean I *can* change things, which means the very future of my existence hangs in the balance.

Unless this Shanna is not actually *my* mom, in *our* past, but instead some kind of parallel-universe version of her. Maybe I can change things in her universe without affecting mine. Maybe, years from now, a parallel-universe version of me will be born, and the parallel-universe Shanna will name her after me.

My head aches with the logistics of it all, with the fears and possibilities.

On Tuesday morning, Grandpa invites me to swim with him again after breakfast. As I attempt to lengthen my strokes and perfect my form into something that resembles his lap-swimming techniques, I realize that the constant music in my head has gone quiet. It never completely goes away—there's always something playing there as long as my eyes are open and I'm seeing colors. But when I swim, I'm able to zone out into the deep blue of the water and *almost* experience true silence.

Even though I can listen to whole symphonies in my head without needing to play the music, I prefer to listen to recordings with headphones, so the music thrums directly into my ears. That way no interruptions or outside noises get through, and I can hear the music with deeper intensity. The colors are so much brighter then, like technicolor.

It's the opposite of this in the pool. The watercolor world is muted, and it's just me and my breath.

In the afternoon, after a few too many hours of loud, colorful silence from my mother and my grandparents, I decide it's time to return to the shed. I feel an almost physical pull that I can't ignore any longer.

I'm not sure if I need to go at a certain time of day to catch Shanna. Is she just . . . waiting for me there? All the time? Or does she only materialize in my presence? Has she been waiting there for days, hoping I would show up and disappointed that I've been avoiding her? Typical that I could've managed to disappoint my mother even before she's become my mother.

As I step over a snoring Vienna to exit the house, my heart races along to Vivaldi's "Summer" from *The Four Seasons* playing in my mind. The pinks, greens, and yellows of the music are all around me in the field.

When I reach the shed I run my hand along the rough outer wall, as if that touch can somehow ground me more than the grass beneath my feet. I close my eyes to listen to the mellow sounds of the gray and brown wood, this time vibrating a minor chord.

I hear her before I see her. Shanna's sobs reverberate black wisps of smoky sound. I nudge the door open and find her there, exactly as I feared.

"Stimpy's gone," she says without even looking up at me. She's sitting on the rough wood floor, her knees bent up and her arms crossed on top of them. She rests her head on her arms and cries into them, her hair cascading around her face.

I'm momentarily frozen, even though I knew this would happen. It's a restatement of theme; this movement of the symphony of Shanna's life has been played before, and unlike the "yes, and" of improv class, the movements can't be rewritten.

Do I dare touch Shanna? If she's a figment of my imagination or some sort of ghost-type entity, would it actually be possible? I'm not even sure if she wants comfort from me. After all, to her I'm just some random near-stranger she's known for a grand total of about forty-five minutes.

Shanna looks up briefly, maybe just to wipe her eyes on the sleeve of her sheer white T-shirt, but our eyes meet, and all my hesitation disappears. I've never been the most comfortable person in social situations, and I've always felt deeply awkward trying to soothe or console people—just ask Julianne. But in this moment, I don't hesitate. I sit down in front of Shanna and throw my arms around her shoulders.

I'm relieved to realize that I *can* touch her—she's not a ghost or an apparition, not a trick of my mind. She's real, in physical form, and I can feel her.

For a moment we just sit there, and I feel the slightest burst of cobalt blue as a tear escapes down my own cheek. I don't need to ask what happened— I already know the story. Mom told me in excruciating detail when I was seven, the last time I ever asked her why we didn't have any pets.

"Who would take care of a pet?" she asked me sharply, a rusty orange chime cutting through the air. "I already have a full-time job, taking care of you and managing your music career! Your dad is always at the hospital. And you cannot disrupt your practice schedule. How would we possibly manage a pet?"

And when I protested—not yet resigned to accepting my mother's first answer as the end—she told me the story of her own childhood pet, Stimpy.

"We didn't have a lot of money," Mom began.

Now, in the sliver of light from the shed's dirty skylight, Shanna doesn't start there. Maybe she's hiding that fact from me, or maybe it's not important to the story in her opinion.

"I had him for twenty-nine days," she says, and I gently rub her arm, massaging small circles of comfort into the cloud-like cotton of her shirt. "He was my responsibility. He was mine. And I let him play in the front yard without a leash on."

I remember Mom saying how her mom, Grandma Florence, told her she could only get a dog if she promised to do everything for it. Mom's sister, Aunt Lily, had no interest in a pet, so it was all on Mom.

Shanna looks at me, our eyes connecting via an invisible thread, before she looks away again, off into the distance in front of her. "My house has this long driveway, with grass on both sides. So I thought I had plenty of room to let Stimpy play on the lawn. He's—he was—so tiny! He couldn't run that fast! Or at least I didn't think he could. But I looked away for *one* second. One! And he made it to the road."

She pauses again to meet my eyes. I nod, letting her tell the story at her own pace.

"There's a pretty busy road at the end of our driveway. Well, it's busy for around here. And . . ."

Mom told me everything she had seen, and how she watched it as if it were happening in slow motion.

"He was hit by a car," Shanna says, and in a memory overlay, I hear Mom saying the exact same words. The same colors, same tones, same rhythm. Like an echo.

Shanna's sobs go from blue to black as they deepen in volume and intensity. I let her rest her head on my shoulder, her tears sinking into my bare skin.

"Shanna, I'm really sorry. What did your parents say?"

Shanna's quiet sniffles morph into full wails, stormy gray-blue like the ocean before a storm. "They said it was my fault. He was my responsibility. And I'm to blame."

I try to reconcile this with my grandparents as they are now: sweet, almost-silent Grandma Florence and low-key, thoughtful Grandpa Jack. How could they blame their daughter—a sensitive, well-meaning girl who loved her dog—for the worst moment of her life up to that point? Why didn't they hold her? Why didn't they just say they were so sorry?

"They both told you it was your fault?"

Shanna's cries slow a bit, and she wipes her eyes on the crook of her elbow. "My mom did," she says. "She doesn't mean to be—I mean, she has these spells. And when she's tired from working all the time, that gets worse."

Grandma Florence? What spells?

Shanna continues. "When it's bad, she can be really mean, but I wish I could fix it."

I can't even wrap my head around having this conversation with my mom, about my grandma. I don't know how to handle this kind of green, open emotion, this kind of honesty.

"So . . . do you get along with your mom?" I ask, not quite knowing how to keep the flow of words going.

Shanna shrugs, wiping her eyes yet again, hiccupping a little as she recovers from crying. "You know how it is. We fight a lot. I guess most mothers and daughters do. Sometimes I hate her but I also just love her so much."

We both lean back against the wall of the shed, and our legs stretch out to exactly the same length, right into the shaft of light projected onto the floor from the skylight. Her green Converse and my flip-flops also appear to be the same size.

"What do you fight about?" I ask.

"Well . . ." Shanna looks up at the skylight and I brace myself, though I'm not sure what for. "Whether or not I was responsible enough for a pet, but I guess she was right about that one."

"No, Shanna," I say, the words spilling out like a rough fountain of turbulent white water. "It's not completely on you. Things happen. Maybe the car was speeding. Maybe someone else should've been teaching you how to take care of the dog. Maybe—"

Shanna shakes her head. "Thanks," she says. "But no. It was my fault, and I'll never forgive myself."

Once again, tears gather in her brown eyes and threaten to fall. Mom always urges me not to cry when I'm upset. Like when I messed up a few notes of a solo in Handel's Sonata no. 3, and afterward she told me to keep it together so as not to draw attention to my mistakes, but I just wanted five minutes of the relief of letting the tears out.

So I don't tell Shanna not to cry, but I do ask what else she and her mother fight about. Now I just have to know.

"My bat mitzvah," she says right away, rolling her eyes. "That's a big one. We fight a ton about that. She won't let me get out of it."

"Why?" I ask, surprised.

Shanna laughs. It's purple, but not a gentle purple. It's an angry color. "Because we're Jewish and it's what everyone Jewish does. I've been going to Hebrew school forever, and it's just what you do next."

I peer at her, her face lit up in the streaming sunshine from above us. "But you don't want to?"

Shanna takes a deep breath and lets it out before answering me. "I don't even know. Sometimes it feels like, if I had a choice, maybe I would choose to do it. But I don't have a choice."

I feel my blood run cold. Sometimes that's exactly how I feel about music, about the violin specifically.

I'm sure my face is a pale gray, and I'm grateful that Shanna keeps talking so I don't have to say anything.

"My mom is weird about being Jewish, because of everything her family had to go through."

What does that mean? I search my memories, wondering what Grandma Florence's parents were like. I can't even remember their names at the moment. I'm not sure I know anything about them. "What did they go through?"

"The Holocaust," she says as if it's obvious. "My mom was born in a displaced persons' camp after the war ended, because her parents met in Auschwitz."

I've never heard anyone in my family mention anything like that. Of course I know what the Holocaust is—I know that millions and millions of people, including six million Jews, were killed by the Nazis in concentration camps like Auschwitz, and that lots of people lost their entire families. I know that Mom's ancestors came to the United States from Europe sometime after World War II. I know Mom's ancestors were all Jewish. But I never knew Grandma Florence's parents met in a Nazi death camp, or that Grandma Florence was born in another kind of camp.

Instinctively I shake my head. "No, I don't— that's not right," I say before thinking better of it.

Shanna stiffens. "What do you mean, it's not right?"

I feel trapped. So far, it's been surprisingly easy to avoid revealing my identity to Shanna. She hasn't asked why I'm on her parents' property or why she's never seen me outside of the shed. It's like there's an unspoken rule that she won't ask probing questions and I won't volunteer certain information. So how can I explain that we share a family, and thus a family history, and that she must have something wrong about it?

I can't say that. I'm going to have to let it go for now.

I backtrack. "Oh, nothing. I'm sorry. I don't know what—" And now I know how to possibly fix it. "I meant that it's not right, like it's not fair. That your grandparents were in Auschwitz." I bite my lip and hold my breath, hoping I've saved the conversation, like I did the first time with the *How do you say what year it is?* school project lie.

Shanna nods. I breathe a misty sigh of relief, pink in the air, mingling with Shanna's previous angry purple, making a color so much calmer and warmer in its magenta magic.

"I'm really sorry about your dog," I say after a long, comfortable silence. "And I don't think it's your fault."

Shanna smiles, though it's a limp half-smile. "Well, I do. But thanks."

I want to ask her a billion more questions, but I'm terrified of endangering our fragile existence.

"I have to go," I say eventually, watching a cloud pass somewhere above the skylight, dimming the shed for a few moments.

"I know," she says, and I have no idea what that means. We stand, and I give her another hug. She holds me tightly, and I wonder again who she thinks I am, or where she thinks I exist.

CHAPTER 8

forte: strong, loud

"**G**randpa," I say later that day while we're both reading in the sunroom, "we're—I mean, you're Jewish, right?"

It's a weird question to ask. I know that my whole family is Jewish. But I don't know much beyond that. I don't know what it *means*. I've been thinking about this since my latest talk with Shanna. I want to ask Grandpa how he *feels* about being Jewish, but I don't know how to put that question into words. I'm sure there's the equivalent of a musical prelude to start the conversation—something meandering and delicate—but I'm not sure how to do that. So I jump in strong, like a first movement that starts off *fortissimo*, like Beethoven's Fifth.

Grandpa puts the newspaper down on his lap.

"With a name like Yakov Goldberg? Yes, I'm Jewish." He chuckles to himself like this is some kind of joke, but I don't really get it.

"Yakov? I thought your name was Jack."

He chuckles again, a tinny copper color that I realize now is more awkward than amused. "Well, it is. And it isn't. My parents gave me a Hebrew name, Yakov. In English, people would pronounce it Jacob, which somehow became Jack when I was little, and eventually it was just easier to go by Jack."

Vienna stirs on the corner of the couch where she's parked next to me. I barely notice her smells anymore, and I'm trying not to be afraid of her. She hasn't tried to bite anyone the whole time we've been here, and even though her slobber is kind of gross, it's kind of nice when she curls up near me and I can feel the vibrations of her breathing, like a lullaby.

"Do I have a Hebrew name?" I ask.

"Of course," he says. "Zehava. It means *golden*."

I sit up straight, even more confused and even more curious than before. "Wait, like my first name?"

Grandpa stands up and walks to the shelf full of family photo albums. He grabs one and sits down next to me, on my other side, careful not to disturb where Vienna's head is resting against my arm.

"Let's see," he says. "Here we go." He points his curled finger to a page with a photo I've seen at home. It's my parents, holding me as a newborn. They look happy. And even though everyone says babies are exhausting, somehow Mom and Dad look much less weary than they do now.

On the next page, there's a certificate that's filled out in a mix of English and Hebrew. "We kept this because your parents didn't want it, but . . ." Grandpa trails off.

I read more closely. Most of it's a mystery, like music written on a different clef. Violins play on treble, and I know some piano, which uses treble and bass, but alto clef, the one violas use, is foreign to me—like the Hebrew writing.

I pick out enough English to get the gist: *A new Jewish daughter has been born.* "Is this like a birth certificate?"

"A naming certificate. You had a naming ceremony when you were a few months old. It's a Jewish tradition. Boys have a bris, a ritual circumcision, but for girls there's nothing like that, so some people have a rabbi come to bless the baby and announce their Hebrew name."

He turns the page of the album, and I see exactly

what he's described. A rabbi, a woman with long dark hair, holds a book open while my grandparents hold me and my parents look on from the side. We're outdoors, in a yard I don't recognize. Probably the house my parents lived in before the one we moved into when I was three.

Dad's parents both died while he was in college, and I know Aunt Lily already lived in Austria at this point, so it looks like it was just the six of us there— my parents, my grandparents, the rabbi, and me.

"How come I've never seen this before?" I ask in wonderment. It's like discovering a whole new color, a new sound I didn't know to look for.

Grandpa's eyes turn stormy gray for a moment. "Your grandmother and I wanted this ceremony for you. Your parents were kind enough to oblige because it mattered so much to us."

I frown, staring at the photo of a major part of my life I never knew existed. "But not to them," I say quietly.

Grandpa nods. "Not so much to them."

"So that's why you have the certificate."

Grandpa nods again.

"Why wasn't it important to them?" I can't help but ask. It's like this chordal seventh minor chord is ringing in the air and I want to resolve it before ending the song. It feels almost painful to leave it unresolved.

A million different thoughts seem to pass across Grandpa's his face before he finally says, "You should really ask your parents about this one, Zehava, my Golden Rose."

He starts to close the album, but I put a hand on his bony arm. "I want to hear what you have to say about it." I sound like a small child begging for something.

"Talk to your mother," he says, putting the album back on its shelf.

But I know I won't. I've tried before. There are certain things Mom doesn't want to talk about, and this shows all the signs of being one of them.

Our days have formed patterns, nearly identical movements of a somber symphony. Variations on a theme.

Grandpa and I have breakfast early, after the visiting nurse gets here but before Tamar arrives. While Grandpa and I swim, Mom goes grocery shopping or stares at her laptop, doing some kind of research that she doesn't talk about in front of me. Grandpa reads the paper in the sunroom. After lunch, the nurse leaves, so Mom and Grandpa take turns watching Grandma Florence: helping her to the bathroom, giving her food and water, sitting by her while she naps. The three of us eat dinner together and watch TV or a movie before bed. Inevitably, at some point, Mom tells me to spend time with Grandma Florence, and Grandma asks me to play my violin. Every time, I tell her I don't have it with me, which is kind of true, since I don't know where in the house Mom is keeping it.

Vienna's routine is consistent, even if it's slobbery and loud. But oddly, the tone of her snorts and huffs is slowly changing for me, from a disturbing gray to a rather peaceful silver. I've never experienced a sound evolving like that, but then again, I've never spent any significant amount of time with a dog either.

On Wednesday morning, after an almost-silent swim with Grandpa, I'm back at the library. I tell myself I've only come to return my books and get new ones. But one of the many musical tracks in my mind knows—and loudly sings to me—that I'm really going there to watch the improv class again. To watch that boy, Mason, with his floppy hair, and all the other kids in the class who seem to move and think and speak so effortlessly and confidently.

Maybe that's how other people thought I played the violin, but it took a lot of effort for me to look as if it took none at all. I used to practice for at least three hours a day, and most days I had rehearsals or lessons in addition to that. Effortless—ha!

I sneak down the steps to the library's basement after the class is already in session, so I can hover in the hallway without being seen. Today the students are making some kind of human Rube Goldberg machine—each kid getting in line to complete an action in response to the kid before them, creating some kind of improv monster of constant motion. Every time they get to the end of a run of it, they start over, and Mia shouts a command for the next time, like "Faster," or "Slow motion," or "Angry," or "In love." And they match their actions to the direction.

Mason is wearing a turquoise shirt today, and I can't take my eyes off him. I like watching people who are really good at something—like the girl in orchestra who plays the harp or the kids on the soccer team whose drills I sometimes glimpse after school. But this is different. I can't match a tone or vibration to this feeling I have when I watch Mason. I also enjoy watching Ryan, the redhead, and Sunita, with her graceful limbs and almost dancer-like moves, but my eyes keep gravitating back to the melodic vibrations of Mason.

I must be thinking out loud or humming a turquoise palette to myself, because before I know it, everyone in the classroom is looking toward the door, spying me through its window.

"Hello?" Mia says.

I freeze. Maybe if I stay quiet and motionless, they'll go back to what they're doing and I can scurry up the stairs.

"Can I help you?" Mia adds.

Someone pulls gently on the door, and it swings open.

"I'm sorry," I blurt out, the words a pale yellow stain on the blank, white silence of the room.

"No worries. Are you lost?" Mia looks at me kindly. I think of Dr. Sascha and how she would react if she caught some strange person observing our BCS rehearsals. Dr. Sascha would get fierce and protective, I think, but Mia is open and curious.

"I'm . . . not lost, exactly," I say, my eyes skimming over the dozen or so faces trained on mine.

I'm sweating, and I feel more on display than I did when I played the Brandenburg Concerto no. 3 at the Meyerhoff last year. "I was just here, and then I heard your, uh, class? And I was watching." I wish I had a sweatshirt hood to pull over my head, or a hole to bury myself in.

"Come in!" Mia says. "Feel free to watch the rest of the session."

I don't know why I don't just turn and run, but the next thing I know, I'm sitting on a cold metal folding chair on one side of the classroom, and the class has resumed.

I should feel weird and uncomfortable observing now, out in the open, especially having just gotten caught. Instead I start to feel at ease. There's something about the gentle music in the room, the warm tones of fuchsia and magenta enveloping me. The improv exercise is comforting in its repetition. The slight variations of each go-round make me feel like I'm listening to a familiar piece of music played on a different instrument each time.

When class is over, though, I feel awkward again. How do I leave? What do I say to Mia? Do I thank her? Apologize for spying? Ask her if I can come back? No, definitely not that.

"I'm Mia—she/her," Mia says to me as the students gather their bags and backpacks from a table on the other side of the room. Their chatter warms the air from pinks to oranges, and Mia's voice is a sunny yellow when she's not projecting and being The Teacher.

"Oh, hi," I say, trying to match her yellow but coming out a little green. I'm suddenly shy. "I'm Rosie. She/her."

Mia grins, and I know I must've done that correctly. We don't offer up our pronouns in school, but I've seen some musicians do it in interviews or at symphony practice. No one has ever asked me, and I love saying *she/her* out loud.

"So what brings you to our fair library?" Mia asks.

I blush. "I'm in town visiting my grandparents. I just stumbled upon your class, and it's . . ." I'm not sure how to finish the sentence. I settle on "I like watching."

"You're welcome to observe any time. I can't let you participate, because of camp enrollment and library insurance and lots of boring stuff, but you can watch."

I don't know what to say—or rather, I can't make

my voice come out, but I'm sure my face shows how grateful and excited I am.

"She's not old enough either," adds a voice behind me that I recognize as Sunita's.

Mason cuts in as I turn around. "You don't know that."

We're standing in a circle now: Mia, Sunita, Mason, and I.

"Mason," he says to me, holding out his hand. As I shake it, I swear I feel my knees wobble a little.

"I'm Rosie. And I'm twelve." I instantly regret saying that. It sounds so childish.

"Hello, Rosie. I'm Sunita. Want to come outside and have lunch with us?"

I'm relieved my age doesn't deter them. I look over at Mia, the adult in the room, and she laughs. "I don't eat with the students, but you should. They're good kids. I have another class to prepare for. Shakespeare! Feel free to come back and watch that one too."

"Oh, thanks," I say, wondering if it'll be rude if I don't.

Sunita smiles at me in an older-sisterly way. "You don't have to come back for Shakespeare. They're not nearly as cool a group as we are. See you next class, Mia!"

She gestures for me to follow her out the door, and I do. I can feel Mason a few steps behind me.

"So where are you from, Rosie?" Sunita chirps. I notice the leather bag she's slung over one shoulder. It looks expensive. Her clothes are really nice and she basically looks like a model in a fashion magazine. I instantly feel even younger and more unimpressive than I did already, but I answer her anyway.

"Baltimore," I say. "But I'm here for the summer. In Hawthorne, with my grandparents."

"Oh, cool," Mason says, stepping up to walk beside us as we reach the main floor of the library and get past the narrow stairs. "The picnic area's this way. So, do you visit your grandparents a lot?"

As I follow Mason and Sunita through the reference section, I explain that this is the longest I've ever spent with my grandparents. I can see him putting it together: I don't know anybody my own age here. I don't have any friends around. I hope I don't seem too pathetic.

We reach a set of double doors that leads outside. There, the rest of the improv kids are seated at some picnic tables, eating various sandwiches and chips and fruit in the bright, abundant sunshine.

Sunita motions for me to join them at a table

where Ryan has pulled his wheelchair up to one side, and the girl dressed in black is next to him eating hummus and carrots.

"Rosie," Sunita says as I sit down between her and Mason, "this is Francie, and this is Ryan. Ryan, Francie, this is Rosie. She's going to be hanging out with us. She's visiting from Baltimore this summer."

I smile, hoping I look friendly even though I'm not sure I've ever been so nervous. They're just being nice because I got caught spying on them, and, oh my gosh, I'm such a creepy weirdo and I kind of want to disappear, and—

"My cousin lives in Baltimore," Francie says brightly. "What grade are you going into?"

"Seventh," I whisper, hoping that it'll just blend into the brown wood of the table, that they won't make a big deal of my being several years younger than they are.

Mason saves me, offering me a package of chips from his lunch bag, and I decline, but it's enough to get me out of saying more. The conversation shifts to the improv class and Mia and the camp that the class is part of. I listen intently as they discuss their other classes—some of them have sports in the after-noon, some visual arts. I piece together that they all go to the same local public school. Ryan and Mason have been going to this camp together for the past few years, Sunita is new to it, and this is Francie's second year.

"What kinds of activities are you into, Rosie?" Ryan asks me kindly. His eyes are emerald green, and I relax momentarily into the major chords they evoke.

Everyone at the table is looking at me with what appears to be genuine interest. This used to be a simple question; my whole life there's only ever been one answer. So I decide to pretend, to answer as I would've if we'd had this conversation three months ago.

"I play the violin," I say simply.

"Cool," Sunita says. "Francie here plays the viola!"

"Cool," I echo.

"I hate practicing, though," Francie admits with a grin. "My orchestra teacher at school says if I practiced more, I'd play better, but, you know! It's so hard! Do you practice?"

I can't help it. I laugh. "Yeah, I practice."

"How much do you practice a day? Because I get bored after, like, fifteen minutes. I just can't go longer than that."

I shrug, feeling that strange mix of shame and pride rise in my face and ring in my ears, vibrating four hundred and forty times a second, a perfect red A above Middle C. I feel Mason's eyes on me, and I look down at my lap. "I, uh, usually practice three hours a day. And then I also have orchestra rehearsals, lessons twice a week, technique class once a week, and concert prep, so . . ."

I can tell they're all staring at me, but it doesn't feel unkind.

"Wow," says Mason. "You must be really good!"

Sunita chimes in. "Yeah, look at you! Maybe someday you'll get to play at Carnegie Hall!"

"Oh, I have. Twice."

The words tumble out like lava—hot, red, careless and bold. If I'd taken a moment to think, I might've kept them in, though I'm not sure that would've been physically possible. Some of my violin life is imprinted on my brain like the finger-work of a song I will never unlearn.

Silence. Except for the A vibrating strong in my head, now in every possible octave all at once.

Mason whistles. "Go, Rosie!"

The others make admiring noises too. Normally I would be embarrassed, but there's something so sweet about their enthusiasm. It makes me feel warm and blue and proud, with tinges of green and yellow and purple and pink making fireworks behind my eyes.

Kids my age at home don't ever react this way. Maybe because they've all known me forever and it's not news that I've played at Carnegie Hall and at the Meyerhoff and at Boston's Symphony Hall. Or maybe it's just that they don't really know what a big deal it is. *Was.*

Suddenly, I'm struck with heavy brown guilt, extinguishing the fireworks and mashing all the colors together in an ugly jumble. This is a lie now. I don't play anymore.

"Actually," I say, clearing my throat, "I'm kind of taking a break. From the violin."

Sunita nods. "For the summer? That makes sense."

And instead of saving face and leaving it at that, I let the whole thing tumble out. Not like lava this time, but more like a soft beige carpet unrolling in front of me.

"I don't really know. I think—I just need some time to see what else is out there. In life. What other kids do with their time. What it's like to do something else. Or nothing else."

They're nodding sympathetically, all eyes on me.

"Whoa," Ryan says. "That's a lot."

Mason pats my hand on the table, and I feel like I might faint. "Yeah! Good for you."

After that the conversation shifts, like ink drying on paper, the colors going from bold and vibrant to washed out and dry. I'm not even sure what they're talking about; the music in my head swells and swallows up everything around me so that I can barely hear anything else. The colors are intense, like the sun shining down on us.

I snap back to the present only when I hear my name.

"What kind of music do you like, Rosie?"

I struggle to climb out of my head, past the intensity of the loud chords and bright colors. I've never known how to answer this question. Other kids don't want to hear that *Salut d'Amour* is my favorite piece of music but that I'm also partial to Shostakovich's third and fifth symphonies, some of Bach's more obscure work, and baroque string quartets.

"Classical?" I squeak out, as if it's a question. "I don't really know pop music, if that's what you're asking."

Mason lights up like he's just gotten the best idea in the world, and my heart does these figure eights inside my chest.

"We've got to introduce you to some music! Rosie, I'm making you a playlist!" He rattles off a collection of words that might as well be a foreign language. "Okay, I'm thinking 'Waterfalls.' Maybe some other TLC? Alanis? Um, maybe No Doubt, some Smashing Pumpkins." He looks over at Ryan. "What am I missing? A few R&B classics? Is Beastie Boys a bad idea? No, Backstreet Boys! That's good. What else is essential music education?"

Sunita laughs, a sprinkle of sunshine rooting me back into a world I can understand. "You'll have to forgive Mason. He's trapped in the nineteen nineties!"

And just like that, I'm uprooted all over again. He's stuck in the 1990s? *Shanna, time travel, 1994.* It's like when people say they've seen their life flash before their eyes, except mine is a blur of thoughts and music and colors—*1994, time travel, Shanna.*

I look at Mason, shyly avoiding his eyes, focusing instead on his forehead. "You're trapped in the nineties?" I whisper. I'm quietly hyperventilating. The tempo of my breaths races to an out-of-control conductor, waving a baton at superhuman speeds to a *prestissimo* movement of a symphony on fire.

Somebody else, besides me, is in a time loop. I knew I felt drawn to Mason more than the other kids. I feel a pull to him I've never experienced before—and now I know why! We're experiencing some kind of time-bending duet. We're not playing the same instrument, possibly not even the same piece of music, but we're harmonically aligned!

"How did that happen?" I ask. For the first time, I make real, intentional eye contact with Mason and let any flutters of what I previously thought was some kind of silly crush fall away. I stare into his eyes and let the brown melody mingle with mine, the tones the same pitch. "How did you find your way into the nineties?"

Mason returns my stare with equal intensity. All the other sounds and colors and stimuli around us are gone, all the simultaneously playing musical tracks in my brain clearing for a moment until it's just the brown waves of Mason's eyes matching the tune of mine.

"Well," he says, "my dad loves nineties music, so I guess he just kind of always played it for me. And it stuck. I mean, I like some current pop and all, but

I'm mainly a fan of the music my dad has always had on in the car and around the house."

Shanna, time travel . . . No.

The full spectrum of rainbow colors returns to my ears, the regular background music resuming in my brain. The Mason melody stops. I once again hear the traffic and feel the sunlight and the green grass below me, the bench beneath my legs. My heart sinks as I realize how completely wrong I was. Mason is not trapped in a slice of space-time the way that Shanna seems to be. He just likes old music.

"Yeah," Ryan says. "It's all he listens to. We try to introduce him to more current music all the time, right, man? But he won't budge. He loves that nineties sh—"

"Ryan!" Sunita scolds, jokingly covering my ears for a moment. Little does she know that there's more sound inside my head than out.

I'm desperately trying to act normally so nobody realizes how absurdly I misinterpreted the comment about Mason. "It's okay," I tell them. "I've heard that word before."

I try to laugh it off, like that one word is the thing that has me shaken. Like I didn't, for a splendid second, think that I'd found a kindred spirit in

Mason, a fellow time traveler, someone who could help me unravel the mystery of Shanna and tell me what in the world it means.

Soon they're all looking at their phones and talking about time—the regular kind of time, like the minutes before their next camp class rotations, the remaining seconds of lunch, the days until the weekend, the weeks remaining of summer. And I see it for a second: a calendar, round and three-dimensional inside my head. It's like a piece of string in a loop or a wheel, projecting outward into space.

Time is a circle, time is *Da Capo al Coda*. Go back to the beginning and play the whole piece again until the new part. Start the song from the beginning, *Da Capo* says. Play again from the beginning until the concluding passage.

Except what if there is no coda, no *al fine*? What if you find yourself just replaying in an infinite loop? Maybe that's what Shanna and I are doing—playing the same piece of music over and over until we get it right. Except I don't even know what "getting it right" means in this situation. With violin, it's playing without mistakes, avoiding dissonance, achieving perfect harmony. With Shanna . . .

I close my eyes, but it makes no difference. I can

still hear all the music. There is no way to stop the music in my brain.

"Will we see you on Friday?" Sunita is asking me. Everyone else has either stood or, in Ryan's case, moved away from the table toward the path that leads back inside the library.

Time is a circle. The months hover before my eyes—September the furthest thing away, the remaining months of summer looming in front of me. I need to fill that time with something besides the bizarre vortex of that shed.

"Yeah," I say. "I'll be back on Friday for sure."

CHAPTER 9

dissonante: clashing, harsh, unpleasant; notes that do not sound or feel pleasing together

Mom wants to take me to a museum. It's Thursday morning, after my breakfast-and-swim with Grandpa, when Mom declares, "I need a change of pace. Dad, you can sit with Mom till we get back, yes? I'm taking Rosie to the art museum."

She doesn't really *ask* either of us, she just declares that this is what will happen. Grandpa will move his schedule around to sit with Grandma Florence, I will go with her even though I've told her a million times I don't like museums.

The truth is I hate museums. They're so loud for me. All the images transpose themselves into music, competing symphonies playing concurrently in my brain, until my head hurts from all the stimulation.

But I don't know how to say no to Mom in situations like this. She never asks the questions, so I don't have a chance to answer. And in a world where I have to pick my battles carefully, I've put my foot down about playing the violin. Every other battle is a small one to concede.

My hair is still damp from swimming, leaving a water spot on the back of the light blue dress Mom insists I wear for this outing. As soon as we get in the car to head to the museum, I can practically feel the oppressively air-conditioned building, the loud colors of the artwork, the frigid white walls, and the headache I'll develop.

"So," Mom says once we're out on the main road, "how is it going so far? This visit. How are you enjoying your time in Connecticut?"

It's as if she's the concierge of a hotel and I'm a guest. Is this how mothers are supposed to talk to their daughters?

"It's okay, I guess."

Mom stares straight ahead at the road. "You barely talk to your grandmother."

I look at her—the freckles on her right cheek, the crinkly lines around her right eye. The half of her I can see is covered in dappled sunlight.

"Am I supposed to?"

"That's why we're here. To be with your grandmother."

"But . . . she can't really . . . communicate," I say quietly. Once again, I feel like I've disappointed my mother because I didn't understand the instructions. Or really, I didn't know there *were* instructions.

We're quiet for a moment. She has no retort.

After a while, Mom says, "Your dad is coming up for the weekend. He'll get in late tomorrow night, after you're asleep."

"That's great," I say, and I mean it, even though I know I sound lukewarm. Of course I'll be glad to see Dad. Of course I want him to come be with us. He's used to dealing with sick people. Even though he doesn't treat Alzheimer's, maybe he'll do a better job than Mom of telling me what's going on, what to expect, how to process it. How to feel.

Suddenly it hits me again that my mom, this woman here driving the car, is also, somehow, Shanna in the shed. I think back over our most recent conversation, replaying it like the recording of a piece of music.

"Mom? Did you have a bat mitzvah?"

The car lurches almost imperceptibly to the left

before Mom rights it and regains her composure. "Why do you ask?"

Because your twelve-year-old self mentioned it, I want to say. "I was looking at old pictures." It's not a lie. I did see those pictures Grandpa showed me. None of them were of Mom's bat mitzvah, because I hadn't thought to look for those yet.

"So then you know the answer," she says.

I roll my eyes, facing the window so she can't see. "Okay, but can you tell me about it?"

She shrugs without removing her hands from the wheel. "It was a bat mitzvah. You know—you've been to a few. It was a Saturday morning, I read from the Torah, a handful of relatives came over to the house for lunch afterward, and that was it."

Dr. Sascha would call Mom's answer "playing the song with a flat affect," which is what she says when I don't pour enough emotion into a piece. Dr. Sascha insists that just getting the notes right is never enough. You have to feel something.

"But what was it like?" I press. "Did you *like* having a bat mitzvah? What did it feel like?"

She puts on her turn signal to make a left into the parking lot of the Coastal Connecticut Contemporary Art Museum. "I had a bat mitzvah because it meant a lot to my parents. I learned the parts I was supposed to know, and I did my best."

She parks near the building's entrance and turns off the car, giving me a pointed look. "Sometimes we do things that aren't all that important to us because they matter to the people we love."

"Are you talking about me and the violin?" I ask, feeling like I've been punched in the gut. Is that what she thinks? That I'm on strike from the violin because I don't care enough about *her*?

"I'm talking about everything and nothing," she says, unbuckling her seat belt. "Being here to take care of Grandma Florence reminds me of all the duties we have to our families."

What about parents' duties to their children? I want to ask. *What about the things we owe ourselves? Why is my violin about you? Why haven't we visited my grandparents more often?*

But I don't ask any of those questions aloud. Instead, as we walk toward the museum's huge wooden double doors, I ask, "What was Grandma Florence like as a mom?"

Shanna said she had "spells." I wonder if Mom will tell me that part or if I'll have to go back to the shed to learn more.

"She did her best. She worked a lot, and when she was home she was often tired. She wanted us to have everything she didn't, and she gave Lily and me as much as she could."

My curiosity is overwhelming. "What didn't she have? What did she give you?"

A big sigh gusts from her lips, cold and blue like ice. "Can we talk about this another time? I just want to enjoy the museum."

It's every bit as loud as I knew it would be. The main exhibit is full of paintings of nature—flowers and the ocean and boats and lighthouses, trees and fields and rivers. Everything explodes with intensely vivid colors and sounds, and I don't want to be here at all.

But since I can't tune anything out, I don't miss it when Mom mutters something under her breath. We're standing in front of yet another loud coastal scene bursting with major chords, about forty-five minutes into our visit, when she whispers, "Almost like a song, you know? So bright and melodic."

I stiffen, scared to even breathe. "What did you say?"

She glances over at me, startled. "What? Did I say something?"

I squint, trying to decide if she's being sarcastic or if she really doesn't realize she spoke out loud. "Mom?"

"Yeah?" She's distracted, looking back at the painting.

"Can you hear that?"

She still doesn't look at me. "Hear what?"

"The music," I whisper, scared to hear the answer either way. I hold my breath.

Mom looks around, searching for a physical music source, and my heart deflates a bit.

"Nope," she says. "I don't hear anything."

Of course, I've often wondered if Mom hears colors too. Or if she sees music in paintings or if everyday sights evoke music in her ears. I've tried to ask her a few ways over the years, but I never ask directly. Because I already know how she feels about what my brain can do. The full truth of how it works would strike her as weird, wrong, possibly even dangerous.

I'm supposed to use it to play the violin and be a musician and impress everyone and be the perfect prodigy daughter. But I'm not supposed to let everyone know just *how* different I am. Some gifts are to be shared, and some are kept secret, even from my mother.

By the time we leave, I have a massive headache. I close my eyes on the drive back to Grandma and Grandpa's house, grateful that Mom doesn't try to start a conversation.

When she stops the car in the driveway, I say politely, "Thanks for taking me to the museum," followed by "I'm going to take a walk."

I'm at the shed in minutes, and I hope that Shanna will be there too. She hasn't failed me yet, but I still don't quite understand how this works—how she's there whenever I am.

I follow the little ritual I've created: I pause by the outside the shed, feel the grass on my ankles to ground me, feel the wall of the shed to center myself, and push the door open, with the creaking *glissando* that now reminds me of a bell above the entrance to a shop.

Shanna's there as soon as my eyes adjust to the light inside. I'm still not sure if she exists here all the time, or if my presence summons her somehow, or if she always just happens to enter the shed in her world just before I enter it in mine. I've never seen her walk in, just as I've never seen her leave.

"Hi," she says, sounding a little bashful—a minty green full of hesitancy.

I remember that the last time I saw her here was right after Stimpy died. Is she embarrassed about how upset she was then? She shouldn't be.

"How are you?" I ask, wondering what direction her answer will take. Will we talk more about Stimpy? Will she say something about how exhausting and scary it is to travel through time?

"I'm better, thanks," she says, and I know she's talking about her puppy. "Or at least I'm getting better. My heart is still broken, but . . ." She trails off, and I reach out and squeeze her hand. It's not something I would normally do for either my friends or my mom, but somehow with Shanna, it feels easy and natural.

There's a long pause before I can't hold it in anymore. "Can I ask you a question?"

Shanna shrugs. "Sure."

I sit down on the floor like we did last time, and she sits across from me, her legs folded under her like a pretzel.

"Why don't you want to have a bat mitzvah?"

"I don't know," Shanna begins, looking up at the skylight. "It's not that I don't want to have a bat mitzvah, exactly. It's just that, like, there are other things I'd rather do."

I feel my eyebrows shoot up. "Like what?"

"Well, I've always wanted to play an instrument, you know?"

No, I didn't know. I had no idea my mother ever wanted to play an instrument. And I don't know the feeling of *wanting* to play an instrument, because I've *been* playing one for as long as I can remember.

"Like the violin or something. A stringed instrument," she continues. "But my mom's always said we don't have time or money for lessons and stuff. So I'm just like, if we're spending all our time and money on Hebrew school and lessons with the cantor to learn my haftorah portion, and food for the party after the ceremony and all that, then why couldn't I just get to use all that for the violin instead of having the bat mitzvah, you know?"

I stare at her, at the tiny freckles on her cheeks that will one day become the larger freckles on my mother's face. The hair she will learn to blow out, the eyebrows she will have professionally shaped a few times a year, the ears she will pierce.

"What?" Shanna says, waving her hands in front of my eyes. "You're staring at me, you're being creepy."

"Oh, sorry," I say, trying to laugh it off. But this is big. This is not what I expected at all. "I guess I just zoned out for a second."

"What about you?" Shanna asks. "Do you play an instrument?"

I laugh again, quieting when I realize that, of course, she actually doesn't know. "I do. I did. Or maybe I still do. I mean, of course I still know how, I just . . ." Shanna is giving me the weirdest look, and I don't blame her. "I play the violin. But I'm taking a break from it right now."

"Why?" Shanna asks.

I take a deep breath. "Well, it's kind of—I mean, it was the only thing I did. And I just wanted to take a break."

Now it's Shanna's turn to stare at me. "I don't get it. Why?"

"It's a lot of pressure," I blurt out, before thinking about how Shanna will one day be my mother, the person who has never once asked "Why?" in all our arguments about this topic. I can't help but wonder if what I say to Shanna now could possibly change the future. If I explain it well enough, will I return to the house this evening and find Mom full of understanding, totally okay with my violin strike?

"What do you mean?" she asks. "Why is it pressure?"

I bite my lip. "Well, my parents . . . they've invested a lot in me playing the violin. It's, like, a whole thing."

"Like me and school," Shanna says, her voice rising from orange to fuchsia, becoming more intense with understanding. "They're big on me getting the best possible grades so I can get scholarships for college."

"Yeah," I say, "kind of like that." It's not exactly the same, though. I don't know how to describe what it's like for me or how much to tell Shanna.

"And like my bat mitzvah," she says. "There's so much pressure on me about that."

I think of Grandpa and the photos of my baby naming. "So your parents want you to have one because of, like, tradition? Because they had them and their parents had them and . . . ?"

Shanna laughs. "Well, my mom didn't have one. Girls didn't have bat mitzvahs back then. I mean, maybe some did, but not her. It's actually more about the people in our family who *couldn't* have them. Like, back when my grandparents' families lived in Europe, they couldn't be Jewish in public. They missed out on a lot of traditional Jewish things. So now Lily and I are supposed to make up for that, I guess."

I study her. "And you said they were in a concentration camp, right?" How had I just glossed over this? The idea that my great-grandparents were Holocaust survivors and I . . . never knew that?

I doubted Shanna last time. I figured she was wrong, confused. But I know nothing about where Grandma Florence was born, I know nothing about her parents.

"Yeah, Auschwitz," Shanna says again. "Most of them died, but that's where my grandparents met."

"Does . . ." I don't even really know what I want to ask her. "Does your mom talk about that stuff?"

Shanna rolls her eyes. "All the time. She's constantly telling me how lucky I am, how good I have it, how easy my life is."

I want to tell her that she'll be saying all that stuff to her daughter—to me!—one day, but of course I don't.

"She's also sad a lot," Shanna blurts out.

"What do you mean?"

Shanna looks away, staring out at the wall. "Most days when she gets home from work, she gets right into bed." *She has these spells,* Shanna said before.

"That sounds really hard," I say.

Shanna smiles a little. "Lily picks up a lot of the slack—she's seventeen, so she cooks and does grocery shopping, and then my dad gets home and tries to make us laugh and cheer everyone up. But a lot of the time, my mom doesn't want to be cheered up. Or she can't be."

"I'm sorry," I say. I can picture it all pretty easily. Grandma Florence, upstairs in her bed. Just like she is now, but younger. My mom and her sister and Grandpa Jack, downstairs in that house, trying to pretend everything's okay. Now it's Mom, Grandpa Jack, and me rattling around downstairs while Grandma Florence is up in her bed. Like some kind of fairy tale. I imagine her trapped there, trapped inside her own brain, unable to get out. Unable to say anything.

"Thanks. It . . . scares me sometimes." Shanna's smile wavers. "Losing her is my biggest fear," she whispers.

I can't even let myself think about how this—her biggest fear—is happening right now in the house up the hill. How my mom, the grown-up version of this girl in front of me, is living out the very thing she dreads the most. I can't let myself go there.

"My best friend—" I stop myself and start again. "My former best friend, Julianne, lost her dad about a year ago."

Shanna's face goes dark. "That's so horrible."

I nod. "Cancer," I say.

"So sad," says Shanna. "Is your friend doing okay?"

"Yeah, she's okay. I think. I mean, I know it's been hard. I guess I don't really ask her about it. Or I didn't. Maybe I should've."

We sit in silence for a long time. I think about how I didn't know how to ask Julianne about her dad's death, about whether she wanted to talk about him. One of many ways I've failed Julianne.

My thoughts turn back to Shanna, to what she said about her own mother. "Why do you think she's so sad? Your mom, I mean."

"I wish I knew. I wish I could make her feel better."

My heart breaks a little for Shanna. She looks like she's holding the world on her shoulders.

"It's not your job to make her happy," I say.

She looks at me, tears sparkling in her eyes like tiny eighth notes at the top of the scale, glittering high and bright and white. "Isn't it, though?"

"You're just a kid!" I say.

She is most definitely not a kid in my life outside this shed. But she was. She is, in this moment.

People have also said that phrase to me—conductors and composers and other musicians—after hearing me play the violin. *Wow, and you're just a kid!* Like my playing is all the better because of my young age. And I never know what to say, because, yeah, technically I'm just a kid, but I never feel like one for real.

I can't ask Shanna if she feels the same way. It's too hard to explain, too close to the truth of how she—future she—has made me feel exactly like she's feeling now. Even though I'm pretty sure that twelve-year-old Shanna wouldn't have wanted that at all.

"Do you and *your* mom get along?" Shanna asks suddenly.

Our eyes meet, and I want to be honest with her. Maybe this is my chance to tell my mother, in some form, something I've always wanted to say.

"Not really," I admit. "I mean, I love her. She'd do anything for me, I know that. But I feel like she only loves me for what I do, not for who I am."

Shanna cocks her head to the side. "And who are you?"

"I guess I don't even know," I say, looking down at my fingers with their fading calluses from the violin strings. "That's the thing. I just want the chance to figure it out."

♪

Later, once I've said goodbye to Shanna and started walking back toward the house, I turn it all over in my mind like a fugue—trying to sort out my thoughts like the multiple crisscrossing themes of the music. Aunt Lily, who took care of her family as a teenager, moved far away as soon as she finished high school. Grandma Florence had spells and stayed in bed most of the time. Shanna felt like it was her job to fix it. All the things I never knew, things no one talks about.

Mom and I have only really ever talked about music. All this time I've spent playing the violin and going to lessons and rehearsing for symphonies—what else have I missed? What else don't I know?

CHAPTER 10

sans nuances: without subtle shades
or variations

Vienna is waiting for me at the doors to the sun-room when I get up to the house. I haven't been inside since we left for the art museum earlier in the day, and now I'm tired and hungry. It's almost time for dinner. After that, I'll read and go to bed and wake up and have breakfast and swim with Grandpa. Time is a circle.

Vienna wags her tail, and instead of cowering I move toward her, my hand extended. She sniffs it and then rubs her side against my leg.

"You're going to knock me over, girl," I say, laughing and gripping the side of the sofa. Maybe that's what she wanted—not for me to actually fall over, but for me to sit down on the couch. I do, and she curls up next to me, her head in my lap. I . . . don't mind it that much.

I pat her and scratch behind her ears.

"Well, look who's finally home," says Grandpa, walking into the room with a book in one hand and a glass of wine in the other. "What adventures has my girl been on today?"

I wonder for a second if he's talking about the dog, but he's meeting my eyes with a grin, so I know he's asking me.

"Oh, you know," I say. "Art museum. Outside. I've been around."

"Your mother's upstairs with your grandma. The visiting nurse left a while ago. Your mom wants you to go say hello before Florence goes to bed."

I look at Vienna: her head resting so comfortably on my lap, her eyes beginning to close as she makes all her colorful, staccato grunts and snorts.

"I don't want to disturb her," I say, not even sure if I mean the dog or Grandma Florence.

Grandpa pauses, as if he's trying to decide how to respond. Eventually, he says, "I know it's not easy. I know you don't know your grandma that well. And I know she's not really herself anymore. But I do know that, someday, when she's gone, you'll be glad you spent a little time with her. So do it for yourself, if not for her."

"But she . . ." I look down at the dog, now asleep under my hands stroking her silky fur. "She always asks me to play her the violin," I admit.

I can sense Grandpa watching me. "You don't have to do anything you don't want to do. All you have to do is be there. You are enough."

And with that, he leaves the room.

You are enough. It's almost an echo of what I told Shanna about wanting to be loved for who I am, not what I can do. It's as if—no, there's no way. Even if a wish I made in the shed could somehow come true back here, thirty years later, I was talking to my mother, *about* my mother, not about Grandpa. It's more likely that he simply feels my need for acceptance right here, right now, without anything supernatural to nudge him along. Though that does make me wonder if he ever thought to tell his own daughters what he just told me.

♪

Grandma Florence's room is quiet, a pale brown tone echoing into my eyes.

I knock softly on the open door, and Mom turns around. Her face lights up for a second, in a way I haven't seen it in months. At least not directed at me.

"I just came to say hello, but I can go if—"

"No, stay. I'll go see about heating up whatever Tamar made for our dinner," Mom says. She kisses my cheek on her way out—another thing I haven't experienced in months—and I'm alone with Grandma Florence.

"Lily? Is that you?" she asks. "Come closer."

I sit in the chair next to her head. I wish Aunt Lily were actually here, since Grandma Florence seems to constantly be thinking of her. But it occurs to me that she might not recognize the real, grown-up Lily. The Lily who speaks seven languages and travels all over Europe for her job. I don't know exactly what her job is—something to do with archives and preserving artifacts? Mom doesn't talk about Aunt Lily's work much, and I've never pressed for information. But I still know more about her than Grandma Florence probably remembers now.

"It's Rosie, Grandma Florence," I say quietly.

"Ah, my Rosie. Did you bring your violin?"

I shake my head. Suddenly I feel a sadness I didn't know was percolating inside my chest. It's green and blue and gray, like the ocean on a winter day. "I'm sorry, I don't have it with me," I say.

"I just want to hear you play," she says. "Play the one from Hungary."

I wrack my brain for music I know that's by a Hungarian composer or that was written in Hungary, but I come up empty. She's confused. There's no point in trying to figure it out. She probably thinks I'm someone else now.

"Maybe next time," I lie, hoping to make her feel better.

But later that night, as I'm falling asleep, Brahms's Hungarian Dance no. 5 in G minor pops into my head. Could that be what she meant?

As I listen to the strident, robust violins play the opening notes, I think of Grandma Florence, trapped in her bed, and my fingers begin to move as if they're making the notes of the song on the soundboard on my violin, the bow making the tones sing out.

My fingers dance on top of the quilt along with the song in my head, and I realize that I do miss playing. I may want to rebel against everything the violin has come to represent in my life, but I still love the music. I miss taking the sounds from my head and translating them through my hands and into the ears of others. I miss the feeling of releasing some of that constant, vibrant music, letting it seep into the world, easing the pressure of the volume in my brain.

What would be the harm in playing one song? For Grandma Florence. If she's the only person besides me who knows I've played, and she can't reliably speak about it, then it'd be my secret to keep.

♪

"I see you brought lunch this time," Mason declares the next day, and I blush deep crimson.

I debated whether or not I should bring something to eat with me to the library. If I did, it'd seem like I was fully planning to spy on the improv class and expecting to be invited to sit with Sunita and Ryan and Francie and Mason again for lunch. But if I didn't bring food, they'd most likely offer me some of theirs, which would feel far more awkward. So I eventually packed myself a sandwich in the kitchen before heading down Hawthorne Road to the library.

"I came here because I had books to return," I tell Mason unconvincingly. I don't know why I can't just admit that I want to be here, that I absolutely plan to watch the class every Monday, Wednesday, and Friday, and that I want more than anything to keep having lunch with them all.

They've been so kind to me, even though they know I'm much younger than they are. They seem incredibly cool here—their very own "in-crowd" of improv kids—but they don't act like the typical popular kids at school. Maybe at their high schools they're more on the fringes, the kind of nerds who are comfortable with being different, even proud of it. I find myself hoping that's how they see me—a fellow outsider, in a good way—and that's why they've been so welcoming.

Mason's T-shirt today is gray, and it makes his brown eyes glow warm like chords on an acoustic guitar. Outside it's a hot, hazy day, the beginning of what's supposedly going to be a record-breaking heat wave in New England over the next week. I'm so thoroughly frozen from spending almost two hours inside the library basement, first reading and then watching Mia's improv class, that the blast of heat when we step into the library courtyard is a welcome relief.

I sit across from Mason. As much as I liked sitting next to him last time, this way I can more easily study his face. He has sharp features, angular like leaping intervals when you're used to hearing steady scales. He's beautiful—there's no other word for it—and he moves so gracefully and confidently, as if he knows exactly who he is and what he's doing at all times. I'm partly envious, but mostly I'm just smitten.

Julianne used to talk about her crushes all the time. I mean, I'm sure she still does, just not to me, since we're no longer friends. For most of sixth grade she had a crush on one girl or another—first there was Anastasia, then Kelsey. Next she was sure that Alexis was her soulmate, but then Alexis started going out with a seventh grader from another school and the rumor was that they were caught kissing at the movie theater near Trader Joe's, and Julianne acted like she'd been betrayed. I wanted to tell her that having the girl you like kiss someone else isn't exactly like having her cheat on you—I don't think Alexis knew Julianne was even alive—but Julianne takes these things very seriously and very personally.

I didn't understand it then. And even now, though I definitely have what Julianne would call a Category 10 Crush on Mason, I know nothing is ever going to happen between us, so how could I be offended if he dated someone else?

Julianne always said I was too practical.

But here's the thing about Julianne. She's the only person in my life who doesn't understand music. She doesn't speak the language. She listens to pop radio and boy bands, but she doesn't *know music*. And you'd think that would've been a bad thing for me, but it wasn't. She likes me—liked me—for me. Not because I can play Violin Sonata Number Whatever by ear. Not because I got the solo in some particular symphony. She just liked being around me. I can't say that about anyone else in my life. Maybe that's why I didn't understand her crushes. Maybe that's why I'm so practical.

I flicker back into the present to join the conversation happening around me at the table.

"It's impossible," Sunita is saying emphatically. The streaks in her dark hair are now dyed blue, glinting in the sunlight to match her tone, cheerful even as she's arguing.

"Nothing is impossible," Francie mumbles.

Sunita continues. "You cannot make a mistake in improv. When there's no script, nothing is a mistake. Right? Back me up here, boys."

Ryan and Mason look at each other, and Ryan speaks. "I see what you mean, Su, but don't you think that there can still be things that are considered mistakes? Like, if you're on stage doing an improv scene and your pants fall down—"

Sunita shakes her head. "Not a mistake. It becomes canon. It's part of the scene. It's true in the moment, and you go with it."

Mason looks at me, his grin like a glittering *arpeggio*. "I'm with Sunita," he says, but he's still looking at me. "Rosie? What's your take?"

I don't know what to say, but for once I don't feel awkward. I'm on the spot, no violin in my arms to hide behind, but I feel somehow safe. The mood is light and airy, like bubbles, and I know I'm okay, no matter what I say. "Well, I don't have any improv experience, so I don't think I can weigh in."

"You've probably had to improvise on the violin, though, right?" Ryan says, leaning his freckled arms on the table.

"No, it doesn't really work like that."

"Wait, wait, wait," Ryan says. "Wasn't it Miles Davis who said that in improvisation, there are no mistakes? Wasn't he a musician?"

"I'll say," Francie laughs, rolling her eyes, but not unkindly. "He's one of the most famous jazz musicians ever."

I smile. I like the way this conversation is full of different ideas and opinions, yet no one is being mean. "Okay, but jazz music is totally different from classical music."

Mason nods, as if encouraging me to go on. Everyone is watching me with kind eyes.

"I only play classical. And everything has to be played exactly as written, otherwise it's considered a mistake."

Francie sighs. "See, that's why I could never be a serious viola player. I can't take the pressure."

"And because you don't practice," teases Sunita.

Francie laughs. "Sure, there's that too."

I feel bold now, part of the group, so I ask the rest of them, "What do you like to do? Besides improv?"

"Soccer," Sunita says quickly.

"She's really good," Ryan adds. "I swim, and I'm on the school newspaper staff."

We all look at Mason. He shrugs.

"Oh, stop being so modest, Mace," Sunita says, nudging him playfully. My heart lurches. She's flirting with him and he seems to like it.

She looks at me. "Mason is good at *everything*. He's in all the school plays, captain of the baseball team, science nerd, amazing artist, what else?"

Mason blushes ever so slightly. "That's pretty much it."

"Oh, don't leave out 'heartbreaker,'" Francie says. There's an awkward moment where Sunita looks away, and Mason stares down at the table. I wish I could ask what that's all about—if he's already broken Sunita's heart, or if Francie's suggesting he's going to.

Ryan ends the silence. "Well, we have to get going for our afternoon classes."

Francie picks up her viola case, which she's been dragging around with her so the instrument won't overheat in her car. I stare at it for a moment, remembering last night, when my fingers ached to play the violin—just for fun.

"I guess I'll see you all around," I say, standing up.

"Are you coming on Monday?" Mason asks. He looks right at me, and I know I can't say no. I nod.

"See you then," he says. My heart does a little dance—somewhere between a waltz and a jig, fast and pink and red.

I watch them all walk back into the library. Francie and Ryan go first, his wheelchair on the smooth asphalt path and Francie alongside him on the grass. Sunita and Mason walk more slowly, and I see Sunita brush arms with Mason, as if by accident, but I bet it's actually on purpose. She likes him. But I can't tell if he likes her back. And I know I'm too young, but I can't help but wonder if Mason would like *me* if only I could travel in time and be seventeen or eighteen or nineteen at the same time as he will be.

CHAPTER 11

obbligato: part of a piece of music that should
not be left out or ignored

Dad arrives late that night, but when I come downstairs on Saturday he's at the breakfast table, having coffee with Grandpa.

"There's my girl," he says, and I give him a hug.
I'm happy to see him, but I can't help missing my
breakfast rituals with Grandpa. We've perfected every
note, every measure. Now Dad comes in like a wood-
wind section that's in tune with the rest of the orchestra but not previously part of this particular piece.

"Have you started playing again?" is the first
thing he asks me. Not "How are you?" or "What
have you been up to?"

Every response that comes to mind is rude. He
knows that if I'd started playing again, he would've

already heard about it. I'm certain he and Mom have a dedicated message thread labeled *Rosie Violin* and Mom updates him constantly, even when he's in surgery. Before this spring, it would've been full of schedule-related things, like the dates of my soloist gig in Pittsburgh or my symphony appearances in Boston, audition schedules for Carnegie Mellon's Junior Virtuoso Competition, Peabody's master classes. Lately, I imagine it's just been a constant back and forth, Dad sending her a single "?" and her replies: a rotating selection of angry, frustrated, and devastated emoji faces.

Grandpa shoots Dad a look that I wish I could capture in a song; it's admonishing and stern but also sympathetic—or maybe sort of wistful? I'm not even sure what color it is—it's not something I've really seen before.

"Rosie and I have been swimming a few times a week," Grandpa says, giving me a wink. "She's got a fierce backstroke."

"And I walk to the library every other day," I add meekly. I don't want Dad to think I'm being lazy.

Dad smiles, but it's just the tightening of his lips, not a complete facial transformation. "Well, I hope you're enjoying this little . . ." He pauses, searching for the word he wants to use to describe my choices. "Detour," he says finally.

After breakfast Grandpa swims, but I don't join him because it's a million degrees outside. The thought of walking all the way to the pool is too much, even if the water would feel good. I sit with Vienna and watch the light make colors dance on the one white wall of the sunroom.

When my parents announce they're going to run some errands and then get lunch, just the two of them, I know what I'm going to do.

Grandpa naps in the afternoons, and as soon as I'm sure he won't hear, I bring Vienna with me into the guest suite where my parents are staying. It's not hard to find my violin; Mom has put it in the walk-in closet, because it's temperature-controlled and has a light-tunnel instead of windows, so the sun can't bake anything inside.

I wasn't sure how I would feel when I finally reunited with my violin. The last time I played it was the day before Julianne announced that we weren't friends anymore, and ever since, I couldn't help but see the violin as part of that problem. Well, as the entire problem. The violin kept me from going to the movies with Julianne on Saturdays. It kept me from sleeping over at her house. It kept me from tak-ing an after-school drama class with her and from being at her dad's funeral.

But I can't be mad at my violin. It's an inanimate object without me. I don't really know who's to blame for all the times I couldn't be with Julianne, but I know it's not the violin. I'm not going back to the way I used to be with music, but I do want to try something now.

I bring the case upstairs, Vienna trailing me. When we get to Grandma Florence's room, she's sitting up in bed and I sigh with relief that she's not asleep. Before I can wonder if she wants Vienna to come in, the dog rushes past me and jumps up on the bed. I wince, worried this'll upset Grandma Florence and ruin not just my plan but the entire afternoon for her. But as Vienna nuzzles up alongside her, Grandma Florence places her shaky left hand on the dog's silky coat, brushing up and down, up and down, and she smiles.

I decide not to wait for her to guess or let her be confused. "Grandma Florence," I say, "it's Rosie."

She doesn't hesitate: "Did you bring your violin this time?"

And even I am surprised at the swell of emotion in my voice as I say, "Yes." My voice, like my name, like my grandparents' last name, is golden.

While Grandma Florence strokes the dog, I kneel down and open the violin case. There it is, my dearest friend, the violin I got when I turned ten.

Before this one, I had several violins: the tiny one I got from a local music shop as a toddler, then the quarter-sized I got around the time I went to kindergarten, the half-sized one I got for my seventh birthday, and the three-quarter-sized one that my parents had made for me in Italy the following year, with a bow imported from France.

But when Agnieszka deemed me ready for a full-sized violin, with a richer sound so that I could truly play with grown-ups in professional symphonies and not just with other children, my parents found this one at an auction house in New York City. It was made in Italy, like my previous violin, but this one is over a hundred years old. It has a deep, throaty tone and all the colors of the spectrum, and as soon as I played it, I knew it was mine.

When I touch it, I feel sparks of electricity run from the smooth, polished wood into my fingertips. They itch with the desire to play. I tighten my bow and apply a fresh coat of rosin to the strings, holding back tears of anticipation and relief.

With the violin nestled below my chin, I feel

more at home than I ever have in any house. With my fingers on the soundboard and my right hand holding the bow, I close my eyes briefly and breathe. It's like a part of my body has been missing, and now, at last, it's reattached.

"I'm going to play you the song from Hungary," I tell Grandma Florence, my eyes still closed.

It's a little rough, since I've never played this Brahms before, and translating songs from inside my head to my fingers can be a process. But it's enough to share with Grandma Florence, for her to recognize the notes. Vienna's ears twitch and I swear she's watching me. Grandma Florence's eyes flutter closed, but she nods in time with the music, a satisfied smile on her face.

When I've finished the movement, Grandma's eyes fly open and meet mine with an intensity I wasn't expecting. It's as if she's fully present for an instant, before her eyes cloud over again and she leans her head back into the pile of pillows.

"That was beautiful," she says quietly. "But that's not the one from Hungary."

I feel unreasonably hurt. "It's Brahms's Hungarian Dance. The fifth one?" That's the one that most people know from the twenty-one songs in the collection.

Grandma Florence looks tired now, her face drooping. "Not Brahms," she says. "The one my mother played in Hungary."

I look around the room, as if some object here is going to translate what Grandma Florence means.

"But that was beautiful," Grandma Florence adds. "Just beautiful."

I nod, trapped between the immense relief and glee of playing again, and the disappointment that this wasn't the piece Grandma Florence asked to hear.

"Can you hum a little bit of the song from Hungary for me?" If Grandma can voice enough of the piece, I'll be able to play it inside my brain and figure out what it is.

She seems to be asleep. So is Vienna, her head on Grandma's chest, rising and falling in perfect rhythm. I'm in the process of packing up my violin when I hear footsteps in the hall.

Grandpa pokes his head in the door.

I'm so relieved it's not my parents that I finally burst. The tears I've been holding in for hours—and possibly since the last time I played the violin?—flow down my cheeks, and my breath comes in uneven gasps like a raging white river.

"What is it?" Grandpa asks in a whisper. He peers

at the bed, seeing Grandma and the dog, and then back at me, his eyes finally falling on my violin case.

Wordlessly, he picks up the case in one hand, puts his other arm around me, and ushers me to my own room.

Once the door is closed behind us, he places the violin case gently on the twin bed that I don't sleep in—the one that's still neatly made up, in contrast to the one across from it where I fitfully toss the covers and pillows around each night.

"Talk to me," he says gently. He sits on the unused bed, and I sit on mine.

"You can't tell my parents," I say first.

Grandpa raises an eyebrow, but he nods.

"She always asks me to play," I say. "And you yourself said I should spend time with her. And I thought maybe it would feel good to play for her."

"But it didn't?"

My crying morphs from the white river to a full ocean, green and gray and brown and blue. "It did, though! It felt nice to play." I catch myself and shake my head. "Not nice. It felt . . . *essential*. It felt like I was breathing deeply for the first time in months."

Grandpa's face softens a bit, but he doesn't move toward me. "Then why are you crying?"

"I don't know. It's just all so much."

We sit there in silence for a few minutes, looking out the window between us onto the field beyond the back terrace. I can't see the shed or the path to the pool, only the blank green grass that leads to two very different parts of my summer life.

"She wanted the song from Hungary," I tell him finally. "Do you know what that means?"

A cloud settles over Grandpa's face, and for a moment I don't even recognize him. "Stay here," he says. He has to duck beneath the sloping walls of the room until he can stand in the center and walk out the door. He returns a few minutes later with a photo album, but it's different from the ones he showed me before. It's older, and the spine's maroon leather has been stitched and then duct-taped together.

He sits down next to me this time, on my bed. "I don't believe in secrets," he says softly. "I don't think secrets are safe or healthy or helpful. But I would appreciate it if you don't mention this album to your parents just yet. Let's call this information a surprise, but not a secret, shall we? Secrets are dangerous, but sometimes surprises are necessary."

I'm not entirely sure what he means, but I nod in agreement.

He opens the album very carefully, as if it's made of dried leaves, and there on the page is a photograph of my mother. Of Shanna.

But no. The eyes are a little different, her body a little longer, her hair not quite right.

"Who is that?" I ask.

Grandpa clears his throat. "That," he says, as if it's hard for him to speak, "is your great-grandmother Dahlia. Florence's mother. Shoshanna's grandmother."

On the next page—I gasp. It takes my breath away. It's another grainy photo of Dahlia. In one hand she's holding a stringed instrument, only partly visible, mostly outside the camera frame. In her other hand she holds a bow. Was Dahlia a violinist?

Grandpa says, "This was sitting in a neighbor's basement in Munkacs for fifty years."

"In where?" I ask.

"The city where Dahlia was born. It belonged to Hungary at the time—now it's part of Ukraine. Your aunt Lily went there and got this album back for us. When Dahlia's family was taken to the concentration camps, a non-Jewish neighbor kept their most precious possessions safe for their return."

I look at him, his blue eyes sharp and wet, a

sound like the violin makes with slides, vibrato, and a minor key—like weeping.

"They never returned. Dahlia was the only one who survived, and by the time the war was over and she was liberated, she was a mother herself, eager to take your grandmother, Florence, to America."

What Shanna told me in the shed—when I insisted she had it wrong—was true. "How did I not know this?"

Grandpa puts an arm around my shoulders gingerly. "Some things are too painful to share. Some memories are best left alone until we're able to tell them as the hard part of a much longer, much more beautiful story."

I think of Grandma Florence in the room down the hall. Of Shanna mentioning her mother's "spells" and talking about why a bat mitzvah was so important to her mother. Of what Dahlia must've gone through.

"Did Dahlia play the song from Hungary?" I ask, tracing my finger over the photograph where Dahlia's fingers wrap around her bow.

Grandpa smiles sadly, his eyes crinkling at the edges. "That I don't know, my Golden Rose. By the time I met your grandmother, so many of her family's stories were locked up in places we could never access, and now anything that remains is locked up again in Florence's brain. I knew your great-grand-mother Dahlia for a few years, but I never heard her play music—or listen to it, for that matter."

"How old was she here?" I ask Grandpa.

He looks up at the ceiling, as if trying to count backward and do the math. "Probably around your age," he says. "A few years later, she was taken to a Jewish ghetto and then to Auschwitz, where she met your great-grandfather. Miraculously, they both managed to survive. From there, they were taken to the displaced persons camp where Florence was born, and eventually the three of them came to New York."

Which paved the way for Aunt Lily and Mom to be born here, and for me to born in Maryland. Dahlia, Florence, Shoshanna, Rosie. We're a chain, each link a different note, a different color, the harmonies of generations.

I tentatively turn the album's pages, staring at more photographs of Dahlia and her family. I take in the way they hold themselves, the expressions on their faces. Sounds swirl in my head, but not so loudly that I can't hear the door opening downstairs.

Grandpa straightens up—he hears it too.

"That'll be your parents coming back," he says. He reaches for the album.

I put one of my hands gently on his. "May I look at this again, later?" I ask.

Grandpa smiles, tucking the album under his arm. "I knew you'd like these photos. When you asked me about time travel, right after you arrived here, I thought of this album. It just took me a few days to locate it, and a while longer to decide it was the right time to share it with you."

Time travel. Time is a circle.

"Maybe," I say, "we could look at it again sometime soon?"

"Of course. And remember," he says, *sotto voce*, from the door frame, "no secrets. Just a surprise for later, okay?"

"No secrets," I repeat. But I do wonder what kind of surprise my mother will think this is when I reveal to her everything I'm learning.

CHAPTER 12

improvvisato: improvised; invented or
arranged offhand

As soon as Grandpa leaves the room, I know I have to get to the shed, where all my questions can be answered. Or at least some of my questions.

For a moment, I wish could bring the photo album to the show Shanna, but two things cross my mind at once: that if something happened to it, I'd be devastated, and that somehow, I sense that I can't bring anything material with me into the shed.

So I go empty-handed, after returning my violin to Mom's room.

"Oh, hi," Shanna says casually once I'm inside the shed. As if she's been hanging out here for hours and I've just coincidentally shown up. I know in my gut that I'm never fully going to understand how this process works, in this precarious place where our time circles intersect.

"What made you want to play music?" I ask her, still winded from running down the meadow to the shed.

Shanna gives me a funny look, head cocked to the side, lips gently pursed, eyes narrowing. I almost laugh, because it's yet another expression I recognize. It's like a familiar song that I'm hearing in a different key when I see it on Shanna.

"Why do you want to know? Where did this come from?"

"I'm having a hard time with my mom," I say. It's something I know she'll relate to—the common ground I can admit to her that we share. I sit on the floor, hoping we can find our easy rhythm like we usually do. My breathing is returning to normal, and I'm relieved when Shanna sits down opposite me, each of us leaning against a wall of the shed.

"Okay, I can definitely sympathize," she says. "But why did you ask about music?"

"Well," I draw out, trying to remember what I've told her, and all the things I have to be sure not to say so as not to mess up the space-time continuum and all that. "Remember how you asked me why I'm taking a break from the violin?"

She nods, her eyes kind and encouraging.

"And I told you that my parents put a lot of pressure on me about music?"

Another nod.

I lean back and try to get comfortable, but my body feels full of pins and needles. All I can think is, *Will she remember this in thirty years? Will it change her? Will it change the way she treats me?*

"I just—I never got to choose music. Music chose me. And then my parents kept choosing it, every day, for me. I guess that makes me wonder why you wish you could play a musical instrument."

Shanna's eyes dart toward the skylight and back toward me. "It's not that complicated—lots of people at my school play instruments. It's just one of those things people do." Her words are orange and resolute.

But she's holding something back. I know it because I see *that* look on my mother all the time.

"Well, kids can do all kinds of things. I bet plenty of your classmates play soccer and do art and"—I think of Mason and fight off a blush—"do improv and stuff, but you said specifically that you would play music if you could."

Shanna shakes her head, and when she speaks, the colors change from orange to pink. It's a subtle shift, but I hear the softening in her words. "I just think I might be good at it, you know? I know lots of people *like* music, but I . . ."

You hear it in colors, I want to say. *You can see the music!*

"My grandmother was a musician, before the Holocaust. My mom's mother. From what I hear, she was really, really good. If there hadn't been a war—if she hadn't been Jewish . . ."

Neither of us breathes. I think of the photo album. I think of Shanna, growing up to be determined that her daughter will play the violin. That *I* will play the violin.

"What was her name?" I ask quietly.

"Dahlia," she says, her smile a genuine one I've only seen a handful of times, in either timeline. "Dahlia Klein. And that's how I'd, like, honor her, if I could. By learning to play an instrument."

I can almost hear the music that Shanna must be imagining in her head. I both want to and don't want to know the answer to my next question. "Wouldn't your parents like that? Since they're so into tradition?"

"No," Shanna says quickly. "My mom barely even likes to listen to music. She told me once that Grandma Dahlia never played again after the war, after her whole family was killed in Auschwitz. She said music was over for her."

This hits me in the chest as if I've been punched for real. I've said the same thing to myself so many times over the past few months: *Maybe music is over for me.*

"So music was over for your grandmother," I say softly, trying to keep my words a soothing blue and not upset Shanna or reveal too much. "And your mom never even listens to music."

"Well, rarely. There is this song that her mother used to hum for her—just a melody, with no words, but I've only heard it a few times. She hums it to herself once in a while."

The song from Hungary, I think. I know. My heart is in my throat as I ask, "Can you—can you sing it for me? Or hum it? Even just a little bit?" The room spins on its axis as I wait, full of white tones and black notes, hoping for her to fill in the colors for me.

Shanna shakes her head immediately. "I'm sorry," she says. "I can't—I can't remember it."

But it's that face again. I know she's holding something back.

I don't know what else to ask her. I don't know what to say. My instinct is to leave. I make an excuse and say a hurried goodbye. I expect my uneasiness to fade once I feel the grass on my ankles and squint in the light outside. But the feeling, like a dissonant chord that hangs in the air far too long, follows me.

Coda. I'll come back to the beginning of this song, hoping that when we get to this part next time, it'll be different.

After dinner—during which Dad describes in excruciating detail the surgery he performed on Thursday—the grown-ups agree to watch a documentary in the living room. I politely excuse myself, saying I'm tired. It's true. But I also just want to think about the pictures in that album, about what the song from Hungary might be.

"I'm going to get in bed and read," I say.

Mom and Grandpa are used to me doing my own thing after dinner here, but Dad, who's leaving tomorrow night to go back to work in Baltimore, looks disappointed.

"Want to come swimming with me and Grandpa

tomorrow morning?" I ask him, hoping this makes up for tonight.

"Grandpa and me," Mom says without even looking up from her crossword puzzle on her iPad.

I'm always disappointing her. "Grandpa and me," I correct.

Grandpa's expression is unreadable, but Dad smiles. "That sounds nice," he says.

In my room, I try to remember the entire photo album from start to finish. I was primarily focused on Dahlia, but there were other people in the photos, people who looked like Dahlia, and thus like Shanna and like me. I wish my weird brain had a photographic memory instead of a perfect auditory memory. If I could copy those images in my mind, I could play them over and over for myself, like a piece of music. But I can't remember nearly enough detail to do that. All I can really see is the black and white, not enough to make music out of it.

I fall asleep and dream that I'm following Dahlia through the streets of Munkacs, but everything is in black and white. I try to call her name but she can't hear me, and the music playing is too quiet to hear because it's not in color. I want to tell her to hide, to avoid the Nazis—and then, once she's safe,

I want to ask her to play me the song. But I also know that if I warn Dahlia about the Nazis, if I alter the history of our family so vastly, she'd never meet my great-grandfather, and Florence would never be born. I would cease to exist.

Dad walks with us to the pool in the morning. It's in the high nineties with what feels like one hundred percent humidity, so a swim probably strikes him as the only sensible activity right now. I can't remember the last time he and Grandpa and I just hung out together. I guess my parents aren't really "hanging out" people. They like to be busy, they like to get things done and accomplish stuff. They like it when I'm doing that too, which is why the violin has always been so helpful. Without it, there's all this empty space to fill.

Dad gasps when we reach the bridge and the clearing. "I haven't been here in so long," he says to no one in particular. "I'd forgotten how beautiful it is." We put our things down on the chairs like we always do, and Dad sits.

"Aren't you going to swim?" I ask him.

Dad smiles. "I'm just going to watch you," he says.

I go over to the deep end and dive in to start my laps. It's easy to pretend Dad's not there—I get into the zone where all the music in my head goes quiet and my thoughts become clear. It's just me and the water, me and my breath. I can not only feel it, I can see it in bubbles under the water when I breathe out.

It's like in winter air, when my breath comes out in white puffs: proof of what my body is doing. When I'm just walking around normally, I have to simply assume that oxygen is entering my body and streams of carbon dioxide are leaving it. I like having visible evidence, like with steam and bubbles. I have that with sound too, though most people don't.

I breeze through my usual twenty-five laps. As I walk up the steps in the shallow end, I can see the vibrations before I can even hear Dad's words, and they make me stop in my tracks.

I know this tone, this mauve color. I know this timbre, and I can't believe I'm hearing it now. It's usually reserved for how he talks about my violin playing, my "career" in music. It takes me a while to actually take in the words, to process how this tone and color are being used outside the context of the violin.

"Rosie! You're a natural! I had no idea you were

such a great swimmer!" Dad wraps me in a towel—and a hug. "You could really do this, you know? If you want to stop playing the violin for good, you could become a swimmer. You're probably too old to get on the Olympic track, but I bet you could swim at a fantastic prep school and get on a college team. Maybe even a partial scholarship! Division One, if you work extra hard!"

Grandpa is out of the pool now too. He starts walking back toward the house, and we follow him, Dad chattering the whole time, spitting gray and lavender and pink to make the familiar mauve.

"I know a guy who coaches at the Baltimore Swim Club—I can call him. We could get you the best private coach, and I'm sure you could catch up to kids your age. You've obviously got the raw talent, and if we really polish up your technique, you could—"

"Dad," I say, still in shock, the purple-gray of his words swirling around me in a screen that makes me feel trapped. "No, it's not like that. I just enjoy swimming."

He squints in the sun as we get past the grove of trees around the bridge. "All the better! If you enjoy it, you'll definitely excel."

"No, Dad." I try to come up with the perfect color, the words that will pierce the fog of his misguided ideas. "I just like swimming with Grandpa, purely for fun. It relaxes me."

Dad stops walking and turns to me. "So you're saying you don't want to become a swimmer?"

I shake my head no.

Dad lets out an exasperated huff. "What is it with you and throwing away everything you're good at? Do you know how lucky you are? And you're just giving it up."

He stares at me with intensity I've only seen from him when I've gone to the hospital with him and watched him telling patients or other doctors about his plans to fix someone's heart.

"People would kill to have the kind of gift you have with music—you're just going to ignore that, pretend it doesn't exist? And fine, so let's say you want a break from music. You're a naturally gifted swimmer—I just saw it with my own eyes—and you're going to quit before you even start?"

He looks truly confused, as if he actually wants some kind of answer. But before I can attempt to explain anything, he goes on, his words a ribbon tightening around my wrists and ankles.

"What if I'd given up my natural gift as a surgeon, huh? What about all the lives I wouldn't have saved, had I given up because not every single moment of being a surgeon is fun or easy?"

"But Dad, I don't save lives with the violin, you know." I'm also pretty sure he wasn't *born* knowing how to operate on someone's heart, but I don't think it'll be helpful to say that.

Before Dad can retort, Grandpa steps in.

"Why don't we all take a break?" he says gently, his words a blanket of blue dissolving the mauve around me. I can breathe again for a moment.

"I have to go," I tell them. I know I'm still in my dripping wet bathing suit. I know I should change. But I also know that if I go back to the house and Mom gets involved in this conversation, it will explode. I can picture the jumble of confetti their words would be—all the colors in the rainbow, mixing to form the murkiest, thickest black-brown until I drown in it.

I'm at the shed before I realize I'm going there, and as soon as I walk in and see Shanna, I burst into tears.

All the yellow sounds I was holding in while my father's words surrounded me spill out as sobs.

"Are you okay?" Shanna asks. She doesn't seem to care that my hair is soaking or that I have a towel wrapped around my waist. She hugs me, and while I thought that would make me feel better, I only feel worse.

How pathetic am I that the only friend I have is an alternate-universe version of *my mother*? How sad is that? My real, actual, forty-whatever mom doesn't even comfort me, so I had to find a twelve-year-old version of her to do it? How unlovable am I?

Shanna begins to hum a tune, weaving together strands of blue and green and silver, and though I'm certain I have never heard it before in my life, I already know it.

The yellow of my sobs weaves in, in perfect harmony, and the music fills the shed.

"Is that the song from Hungary?" I ask, once she's stopped humming and I've stopped crying.

Shanna looks at me, confused. "Is what the song from Hungary?"

"You were just humming something. A song."

Shanna blushes and laughs uncomfortably. "Oh, yeah, I'm always humming under my breath. I never even realize I'm doing it, and then someone will hear me and ask me to stop. My mom hates it, especially when she's having one of her spells and needs absolute silence. But I can't help it, I swear!"

I take her in—her small frame, her innocent eyes full of emotions I can't interpret. She knows things I don't. "That is so sad," I say. "You have a really pretty voice."

"Well . . ." She takes a step back and sits on the floor, gesturing for me to do the same. ". . . at least I'll get to chant my haftorah portion. That's almost like singing. And that's the closest I'll get to music lessons."

I sit too, but I lean forward emphatically. "But if you love music, you should ask your parents for—"

Shanna cuts me off with an all-too-familiar glare. "I don't want to talk about it." A tense moment passes before she asks, "Are you going to tell me why you were crying?"

The tears well up again in my eyes. "Sometimes I hate my parents," I say, not looking at Shanna. It feels strange knowing that she's one of them, but in so many ways, she's not. Yet.

"Join the club," she mutters. "What did yours do this time?"

I swallow hard. "They're obsessed with me being good at one thing. Like, being *the best* at just one thing. And it's been violin my whole life, but suddenly my dad is like, *You could be a Division One swimmer, Rosie! What a great idea!* and I'm just like, no. I want to do some things just for fun, you know?"

Shanna shrugs. I can tell she doesn't really get it.

"And it's probably all just a ploy to make me play the violin again. My dad could've planned it all out. Like, maybe he even had my grandpa get me interested in swimming as a test, to see if I *have what it takes to be the best* or something."

Shanna stares at me with curiosity and amusement. "Wow. Your family sounds . . . interesting."

This makes me laugh, even as more tears spill down my cheeks. "You have no idea."

Shanna tilts her head to the side. "But don't you think—in their own weird way—they're just trying to love you?"

I immediately shake my head. "I don't think that's what love looks like. I feel like they had me just so that I could be their trophy, their prize. They can show me off to the world like, 'Look, we did it, we have a genius prodigy child!' and then everyone will congratulate them as if they had anything to do with it."

"Well, they did create you."

"Yeah, but neither of them practices the violin thirty hours a week."

Shanna musters a small smile. "Well, I'm sorry. I hope they know how lucky they are to have you, just as you are, violin or no violin."

I stare up at the skylights, where clouds are gathering, dimming the sunlight slightly. "How is it you know the right thing to say right now, but in the future . . ."

"In the future, what?" she asks.

I blink and meet her eyes, suddenly aware of what I almost said. "Nothing." I take in and release a huge breath, trying to calm myself.

Once again, we sit in silence. Well, as close to silence as my brain allows. It's furiously replaying the melody Shanna hummed to me earlier.

"Do you want to have a kid someday?" I ask her suddenly. Maybe I shouldn't. Maybe I don't want to know if the answer is no, but I ask before I have a chance to think better of it.

Shanna's face lights up, a perfect major chord. "Of course!" she says. "I want to have, like, four or five kids, so they're never lonely. And I will give them everything I never had. It'll be so much fun. Probably loud and chaotic, but that's what I want."

I feel physical pain in my gut, like I've been punched. How does This Shanna become That Shoshanna? How does all this color and fire drain from her? What happens over those thirty years to dull her light?

I'm so tempted to tell her that her plans don't pan out—warn her that she's not going to have the future she's imagining. But what if I warn her and she decides to take action to make sure she *will* have that? Would it mean she'd marry someone different, someone who also wants a loud, chaotic house full of kids? Would it mean she'd end up with a bunch of kids but none of them would be me?

On the other hand, if I can judge by the Stimpy incident, nothing I say will really change anything for either of us.

"I'm so sorry," I say to Shanna, as I get up and walk toward the door.

She looks at me with confusion. "That you have to go?"

That's, of course, not at all what I meant, but I just nod. And after all, maybe it's better that she doesn't know that things are not going to turn out how she hopes.

Back at the house, something feels off. No one is on the ground floor. No Grandpa reading in the sunroom, no Vienna waiting for me at the door or snoozing in her preferred patch of sunlight. No sign of my parents.

I head upstairs, my pulse pounding in my ears. The steady rhythm—some polka by Strauss I can't quite remember—gathers speed with each step I climb.

I hear Dad first, his doctor voice. It's the most beautiful shade of blue: calm, reassuring, soulful. "Just deep breaths, Florence. Yes, like that."

When I peek around the doorframe, I see him sitting on the edge of Grandma's bed, a stethoscope pressed gently to her back as she sits more or less upright. I know the feel of his hands from the times he's taken care of me when I've been sick. They're smooth and clean, not moist but not too dry, smelling of soap, and just cold enough to be comforting.

I watch him check the glands on her neck and under her chin, all the while speaking to her in that beautiful blue doctor tone.

"Good, just relax your neck. Okay, and look up, and now down. Good."

The blue melody of his voice swells so loudly in my body that it completely obliterates all the angry mauve from earlier. He doesn't have to do this for Grandma Florence. She's not his patient, and even if she were, these kinds of checkups aren't part of his job as a surgeon, any more than it's a conductor's job to tune somebody's instrument. He's doing it simply because he cares. This is the way my father knows how to show love.

How is it that people can be so many versions of themselves? Variations on a theme, movements before the coda. This is who my dad is when no one is watching.

"Hi, Daddy," I say quietly, almost matching his blue with mine.

"Hey, sweetheart," he says, looking up and meeting my eyes.

Arpeggios swell inside me—the chords of missing him already because he's leaving to go home soon, and missing the ease of our relationship back when I just played the violin and did what my parents wanted me to do.

"Hi, Grandma Florence," I say.

"Is that Lily?" she asks, as she often does, her eyes on her quilt.

The *arpeggios* bring me grace and patience. "It's Rosie."

She looks up and finally sees me. "The violin," she murmurs.

I look at Dad, careful not to blurt out anything to Grandma Florence that I don't want him to know: that I've played for her, that I've seen Grandpa's "surprise" photo album, that I'm trying to figure out the song from Hungary.

Dad doesn't seem to register Grandma Florence's words, though. He helps her lie back down on her bed, and she closes her eyes, smiling. He stands up from the bed, his exam complete, and squeezes Grandma's shoulder affectionately.

"Rosie, can I talk to you for a minute?" he says. It's unusual for him to *ask* instead of just declare that he needs to talk to me, and his voice is a kind of aquamarine I have never seen from him before.

I nod and step out into the hall with him.

"I'm sorry I upset you earlier," he says. "Are you okay?"

My love for him surges, uncomplicated and unconditional. I know he doesn't really understand *why* I was upset, but I also know that he didn't mean to hurt me. He wants me to be happy, even if neither of us is sure what that looks like.

"I'm okay," I say. "Where are Mom and Grandpa?"

"I sent them out to get some things your grandmother needs," he says. "A prescription, a new heating pad, a few other supplies from the pharmacy."

"Thank you for taking such good care of her," I tell him.

He smiles sadly. "I wish there were something I could actually do—something anyone could do."

I gesture for him to follow me further down the hallway, away from Grandma Florence's room, and he does. "Is she . . . going to die soon?"

"Yes," he says. His voice is the kind of music that's sad but not tragic. The key you play when a person has lived a full, long life, and when they've had all the care possible and nothing has worked.

He hugs me and I breathe in his simple, familiar smell—laundry detergent and hospital soap and something else that I can never identify.

"I'm going to suggest to your mom and your grandpa that it's time we bring in hospice," he says into my hair.

"What does that mean?" I've heard the word before, stiff and itchy and raw like the palest green burlap.

Dad pulls away so we can look at each other. "It means your grandma has very little time left. Maybe a few weeks, but probably more like days. And the hospice workers can help keep her more comfortable, with pain medicine and whatever else she needs."

I think of the song from Hungary. "Will she still be able to see and hear us?"

Dad nods. "I think so. At least for a while."

I have to get my hands on that photo album again. I have to look for clues. I have to play the song for her, close the loop, complete the circle, and give her the only thing she has ever asked of me.

CHAPTER 13

encore: again; a return to the stage to play a
bonus piece of music

That night, after Dad has left, we eat a quiet, sad dinner in the dining room. Mom and Grandpa talk a
little about the hospice workers who will start showing
up tomorrow morning, and about Aunt Lily's travel
arrangements. Apparently she's having a hard time
booking a flight but will get here as soon as she can.

Mom's eyes are red and watery. *Losing her is my
biggest fear,* Shanna said one time in the shed. And
here we are. We all knew this was coming, but I don't
think any of us were prepared for how it would feel.
It's like this silent house is screaming in muted colors.

When Grandpa and I are cleaning up in the
kitchen, I ask him, "Can I please take another look
that album?"

I haven't seen Grandpa cry, but I know he's full of pain, and I feel a distance between us for the first time in a while.

Still, he nods. "I'll bring it up to your room."

Without thinking, I throw my arms around him and bury my head in his chest, just as I did with Dad a few hours ago.

"Mother Hubbard, that's a strong grip you've got," he says, and I giggle, even though I know we both feel terrible.

"I love you, Grandpa," I say. They're words we've never spoken to each other, at least not that I can remember. I don't know why. It's always in the spaces between the notes of our songs.

He squeezes me tightly. "I love you too, Golden Rosie."

When I leave the kitchen, I find Mom still sitting at the dining room table.

"Oh, Rosie," she says, forcing a smile, "you startled me."

I look for signs of Shanna in her—the softness, the vulnerability, the openness I love about her younger counterpart. But Mom is impenetrable. If not for the redness of her eyes, it'd be hard to tell that she's feeling anything.

"Are you okay?" I ask.

She nods and stands up, wiping her hands on the skirt of her sundress. "Thanks, honey. Good night."

She takes off for her room, and I realize my mistake. For a moment there, I expected her to confide in me like Shanna would've. To admit how hard and scary and confusing this whole experience is.

But Mom always has things under control—or pretends to. There's no room in her life for the messiness that comes with openly sharing your emotions.

It's hard to imagine all the things that must've happened in the years between when she was Shanna and when she is the woman I know now. What hardens someone's heart? What drains out all the curiosity? What kinds of colors and music were taken away?

Grandpa delivers the album, as promised, and drops a good-night kiss on the top of my head. When I'm alone, I turn the pages slowly, lamenting again that the photos are in black and white. But as I stare at image after image—the faces of my ancestors, and of the people they loved and would soon lose—I notice all the myriad shades of gray within the black and white. Slowly but surely, a melody emerges.

The strangest thing is that I start to recognize it.

Because, of course, it's an orchestration of the melody that Shanna hummed earlier in the shed.

Somewhere in her brain are the same patterns I'm finding in the black and white and gray and gray and gray of the photographs. The people of Munkacs take on color in my mind, and the song emerges. Dahlia is the melody, and everyone she loves—the people around her in these pictures—are the harmonies, the variations, the counterpoint, the timbre, the tone.

As soon as I recognize the piece of melody that Shanna hummed in each picture, the shades of gray come to life, as vivid and as varied as any full-color experience I've ever had. Once I know how to hear it, I see the music everywhere, embedded in the images in shadow and light.

"Thank you," I whisper to Dahlia. Page after page, I hum quietly to myself until I know the entire song and all its movements.

Eventually I fall asleep and dream it in a symphony, with hundreds of instruments each playing a unique orchestration, with lights and fancy clothes and a crowd of thousands. But at the root, it's just the melody Shanna didn't know she was humming into my ear. A melody that the Nazis couldn't destroy, that Grandma Florence's brain couldn't erase.

Dahlia and Florence and Shanna and I—we are the sequence, each of us a movement, and the melody flows from one of us to the next. It lives on past hardship and loss, over continents and decades. It transcends death and time. It is a circle, with no beginning or end. And now I know every note.

Finding a time to play the song for Grandma Florence is going to be tricky, I realize the next morning. Grandpa and I are eating breakfast when a hospice nurse named Laura knocks on the door. She's about Mom's age, white with straight blond hair and a very warm smile.

Moments later, two guys bring in a hospital bed and carry it up to Grandma Florence's room. Before I know it, the house is filled with the cacophony of people coming and going, bringing in medicine and machines and melodies.

I'm relieved to have somewhere to escape to—the

library and improv class and Mason and everyone.

As I'm leaving, Mom says, "I'll be meeting with Grandma Florence's doctors this afternoon. Someone from hospice will be here with Grandma, but hopefully she'll be napping, so please don't disturb them until I'm back, okay?"

"Okay," I say, grabbing the sandwich I made. I'm still wondering how I'll find an opportunity to play what I think—what I hope—is the song my great-grandmother played in Hungary.

Mom places a quick, efficient kiss on the top of my head. She doesn't ask where I'm going or check that I've remembered to put sunscreen on or warn me about getting dehydrated. Like the calluses I used to have on my fingers from the violin strings, she's lost a bit of her edge.

Connecticut is experiencing a historic heat wave—today's apparently the hottest day on record for decades. If I had any other option, I wouldn't walk the half mile to the library. Well, staying home is technically an option, but I'm desperate to get a break from the hospice workers and the house and the heavy sadness that's settled over it.

By the time I get to the library, I'm soaked in sweat but grateful that my navy sundress hides the sweat stains. I spend a few minutes in the bathroom, in the path of the air conditioning vent, running ice-cold water over my wrists and splashing it on my face.

When I get downstairs to the theater, Mia is talking to the students about the importance of "staying in the moment" during an improvised scene.

"You can't let your mind wander," she says, pacing in front of the wheeled dry-erase board that sits at one end of the room, "or bring in ideas that you came up with at home on your own. That just doesn't work. You have to let yourself be inspired in the current moment and go from there."

I know people do practice a lot for improv shows, but I can't help feeling a little jealous, comparing that process with the painstaking hours I used to spend rehearsing for violin performances. It seems unfair. Why did my "gift" have to be for something that requires such rigid techniques?

On the other hand, I've only ever played a very particular kind of music. My parents and instructors have led me to believe that there's one purest, highest form of classical music, and that this is the only form worth playing. But I know there are other styles, even within classical music, not to mention all the genres outside of it. I've seen YouTube videos of people playing the violin very differently than I do—klezmer musicians, Celtic fiddlers. There's no reason that playing music can't be flexible and fun, like improv.

The thought catches me off guard, like I'm transitioning mid-song from familiar material to something new. For so long I've been encouraged to see music only one way. What if there's a whole other range of colors and sounds I'm only beginning to hear?

I'm still thinking about this when I follow Mason and everyone out to the lunch area.

"I can't do it," Sunita groans. "It's too hot. Can't we eat inside?"

"The library has a pretty strict policy about food," Ryan points out.

Mason sighs. "I agree with Sunita. It's too hot to eat outside."

"I wish one of us had a pool," Sunita says, coiling her long hair on top of her head and fanning her neck. "What about the community pool?"

"Closed Mondays," Ryan says.

"And the YMCA is being renovated," adds Francie forlornly.

Mason takes an unenthusiastic bite of his sandwich. "Who do we know who has a pool?"

I suddenly find myself saying, "I have a pool." It's technically Grandma and Grandpa's. It's not mine to offer. Still, no one besides Grandpa or me has been in it the entire time I've been visiting, and I know Mom is at the meeting with Grandma Florence's doctors, and Grandpa is usually napping at this time of day. *Yes, and . . .*

Everyone looks at me. Sunita brightens. "OMG, our hero, Rosie!"

I blush, feeling instant regret mixed with the cool yellow of delight.

"Nice," Mason says. "Would you mind if a few of us came and swam?"

"Swam?" Sunita asks. "I think it's . . . swum. Swum? No, that sounds wrong too."

Ryan laughs. "I don't care what you call it. It's so freaking hot and I'm so sweaty. I'd give anything to get out of my chair and float around. I have my suit in the car."

"Me too," Sunita says, jumping up and down and clapping lightly. "Well, in my bag. From when we went to the beach last week."

I look around, wondering if there's a way to back

out now. "Don't you all have afternoon classes?"

Sunita shakes her head. "They've been canceled because they're outdoor sports classes, and the Parks and Rec center decided it's too hot for that."

Francie fans her face. "They're not wrong. Can I bring Taylor too?"

Taylor is another kid in the improv class, and while they don't eat lunch with us, they've always been nice to me and are very funny and talented in class. That'll make five people. Five guests.

All eyes on me, like I'm the conductor and they're waiting for me to lift my arms and start the symphony.

Yes. And.

"Sure, let's do it," I say, without even thinking about the logistics. All I can see is the light in Mason's eyes.

He grins. "Where's your house, Rosie? And who's picking you up?"

I blush again, because Mason is looking at me and it's like a ray of sunshine softly warming my skin in golds and pinks.

"My house is, like, half a mile from here. I usually, um, walk." I've never felt more excited yet more awkward. This is really happening!

"What's the address?" Mason asks, and I tell him. He plugs it into his phone. "I'll drive you. Sunita, you can come in my car too."

My heart only sinks a tiny bit, bobbing back up to the surface just as quickly. I both want and don't want to be alone with Mason. And it's not like I'm surprised that he wants Sunita to join us.

"Then I'll take the rest of you," Ryan says, and Taylor and Francie follow him to his van.

Suddenly, I think about Ryan's wheelchair. It'd be hard for him to get across the bridge and down the steps to the pool area. But we can use the back driveway that runs behind the pool. I'm pretty sure the guy who cleans it parks there and it's never been an issue.

"Text Ryan and tell him to follow you," I tell Mason. "There's a back entrance where we can park closer to the pool." I'm impressed by how confident I sound. I feel like I'm channeling Shanna a bit— acting how I think she'd act with a bunch of friends, including a boy on whom she has a completely impossible crush.

When we get to Mason's car, Sunita sits in the front passenger seat next to Mason, and I try to hide my disappointment. I watch her casually put her hand on his arm while she chatters about how hot it is. She has incredible self-confidence that's a perfect match for his. I can't even be that carefree and fun around Julianne, let alone with someone I'm crushing on.

As we drive down Hawthorne Road, I wonder what Julianne is doing at this very moment. I wish I had a way to tell her that I'm riding in a car with a boy I have an actual, honest-to-goodness crush on. Even though he's older and has no interest in me, Julianne would be impressed. If we were still speaking, and if I had a phone or iPad or any way to reach her.

I guide Mason along the part of the driveway that splits off to loop around the back of the property. We meander through dappled sunlight and tall trees until we get to the clearing and I can see the glint of the pool water. Ryan follows us in his van and parks behind Mason's car.

"Dang," Taylor says as they climb out of the van. "This place is sick! This is your house?" They look at me with awe.

I feel incredibly uncomfortable again, not only with the reaction to how nice the place is, but also with the knowledge that I invited them over without asking any grown-ups. Well, whatever. Mom has basically abandoned me all summer. She has no idea what I'm up to all day, any day. As long as I'm not practicing my violin, what I do doesn't seem to matter to her.

"It's my grandparents' house," I tell Taylor. "I'm just visiting. The pool's right over here."

I show them a gap in the plants that Ryan's wheelchair can fit through, and everybody makes it into the pool area.

"Holy smoke," I hear Francie mumble. "This is sweet!"

"It's truly lovely," Sunita says.

But I barely hear them because I've caught Mason's eye, and he's smiling, and I'm swaddled in turquoise warmth and lemonade-yellow joy.

"Wow, thank you, Rosie," says Mason. "This is so cool."

"Literally," Sunita says, fanning herself.

I have to go up to the house to get my bathing suit and towel, so I leave everyone there to figure out changing on their own. They can do whatever teenagers do about changing in front of each other or not.

Inside, I throw on the first suit I find—a navy-blue

tank suit that's nothing special and only emphasizes the complete flatness of my chest and my lack of hips. I hesitate in the mirror for a moment, wishing I had something fun and flirty, but I just toss my hair into a ponytail and race back outside. Who am I kidding anyway? I am who I am. No cute swimsuit would make me old enough—or cool enough—to win Mason's heart. Also, I'm pretty sure most people don't like other humans just for the kind of bathing suits they wear or for how their hair looks.

I run across the green meadow to the bridge. I can hear splashing and whoops of joy as I cross over into the clearing, and I see that Francie and Taylor are in the water. Sunita and Mason are holding Ryan's chair while he uses his arms to gracefully slide into the deep end of the pool with a splash.

Sunita jumps in cannonball-style, which is kind of a funny contrast to the delicate cuteness of her purple bikini. I stand at the steps of the shallow end, and Mason walks over to join me. He dips a toe in and shivers a tiny bit at the cold, his dark hair falling in front of one eye the way it did that first day I saw him at the library. My heart dips and soars, playing Mozart's *Eine Kleine Nachtmusik* at twice its intended tempo.

"I forgot to mention how cold the water is," I say nervously, searching for a conversation topic. I feel so self-conscious that I wish I could hide myself inside my own skin.

"It's the perfect temperature." Mason winks at me, and *Eine Kleine Nachtmusik* accelerates even more in my head. It's not a romantic wink—more like a brotherly one, I'm sure—but I have literally never felt this happy. I can feel every single nerve dancing, just from the thrill of standing next to him.

I know everyone's just being nice to me because I'm this lonely misfit lurking around the library, and that under normal circumstances we never would've even crossed paths. But I feel so lucky that we do overlap, kind of like how Shanna and I randomly exist in time together every so often.

Mason takes another step into the pool and turns to look at me over his shoulder. "Coming in?"

I grin and move one more step down.

"Let's jump," he says. It's too shallow to really jump in, but on the count of three, we both stretch forward and skim into the pool headfirst, our arms briefly touching as we hit the water's surface.

We both come up for air, and Mason flicks his head so that the long pieces of hair in the front flip backward, out of his eyes, spraying me in the process.

"Thanks for that," I say jokingly, splashing Mason ever-so-gently in retaliation.

Mason's brown eyes twinkle. "Oh, so that's how you want to play it," he says. The next thing I know, he's splashed me with a wall of water in my face.

I laugh and return a huge wave over toward him, but it's too late—he's dived under the surface to avoid it.

We splash back and forth a few times, until Sunita swims over and puts her arms around Mason from behind.

"Water ride!" she commands. Just like that, the moment is over, and Mason swims around the perimeter of the pool with Sunita on his back, laughing in the exact shade of her purple bikini.

I suddenly feel engulfed in the kind of loneliness I thought I would feel all the time this summer—the dark velvety green of missing Julianne and wishing I had someone else in my life I could talk to besides Shanna.

Taylor breaks into my thoughts, swimming up beside me and asking, "Do you have any siblings? Any other kids living here with you this summer?"

I almost laugh, thinking of Shanna and how I would ever explain that. "I spend a lot of time with my grandpa," I settle for saying.

"You must miss your friends at home, though. How long are you here for?"

I smile, wishing I could change the subject or just breathe underwater, anything to get away from talking about this. Everything Taylor says reminds me that these kids here in the pool right now aren't *really* my friends, since they're all older and I don't actually belong.

"Six weeks," I say. My time in Hawthorne is racing by—or maybe it's just been folded in on itself, thanks to my visits to the shed. I duck under the water and stay down there long enough to let my brain go quiet for a few seconds, before I pop up to breathe.

I try to picture Julianne here. In another time-line, if we were still friends, I could imagine her mom letting her come up and stay with us for a week. I would bring her to the pool. I would have her walk to the library with me and introduce her to Mason—casually, of course, just to get her objective opinion of him. We'd play cards in the sunroom, have breakfast with Grandpa, and take Vienna on long walks in the woods. But I wouldn't take her to the shed. Shanna is all mine.

Eventually the group gets out of the pool to dry off in the sun and eat their lunches. I swim a few laps before getting out to join them. I'm not trying to show off my swimming skills or draw attention to myself or anything, but I am delaying having to get out and talk to everyone more. I'm feeling drained from all the social contact, wishing I could disappear into some music for the rest of the afternoon and get carried off into a stream of Bach and Beethoven like I used to.

I miss playing music more than I let myself acknowledge most days. Times like this, when people feel like too much for me, I long for my violin, for the solitude of just it and me, making music together. That's never felt lonely. It's like speaking through the echoes of time and space to the composers. The music they wrote laid out the maps that take me inside their brains, through the pictures they paint of their worlds and their adventures.

Tucked under one of the lounge chairs, I see the unmistakable shape of an instrument case. "Is that your viola?" I ask Francie as I dry off with my towel.

"Yeah, I didn't want it to fry in Ryan's van.

I need it for my music class this afternoon. That's the only time I remember to play at all, honestly."

Suddenly I'm overcome with the need to hold an instrument, even if it's an unfamiliar one.

"Could I play it for a minute?" I ask shyly. I can't believe I'm saying the words out loud, inviting the kind of attention I've been avoiding all summer. But the ache to play music here, in the speckled sunshine of this magical spot, is overwhelming.

"Uh, sure." The rest of the group goes silent as Francie passes me the viola. I take it from its case like a baby from a crib and tighten the bow exactly how I like it. I tune the strings by ear.

I could work on the song for Grandma—my fingers are itching to play it—but that melody feels very, very private and off limits in this company. So I play *Salut d'Amour*, feeling the arches of longing and the ribbons of pastels flow out of my hands, into the viola, and diffuse like droplets into the air.

The viola is a little larger than a violin, and the strings are different, so I have to adjust the music in my head as I play, but it's fairly easy. I'm able to transpose the notes into slightly darker colors to match the instrument's lower tones, and before I even reach the bridge of the song, I feel like I've played the viola for years. So much of my violin technique transfers right over into it. I feel comfortable, but also excited at the newness. A little change feels good.

By the time I play the final note, my eyes are moist with the joy of seeing the music again.

"Holy freaking smokes," breathes Ryan when I lower the bow.

"Good grief," Sunita says, her hand over her chest in reverence.

Francie shakes her head. "It never sounds like that when I play it," she mumbles, but not unkindly.

Mason stares at me. "Rosie," he says, almost whispering, "I had no idea. I mean, we knew you had to be good, since you practice all the time, but . . ." He trails off, looking into my eyes like he can see something in them that no one has ever seen before.

I thought I would feel exposed, playing like this in front of these people I hardly know. But I feel more confident—more comfortable—than I have all day. All month, maybe.

I hand the viola back to Francie. "Thanks for letting me play," I say, loosening the bow so it can be stored safely in its nest.

"That was incredible," Taylor tells me from where they sit on a lounge chair. "You should have a

YouTube channel or a TikTok or something."

I laugh. Normally, with kids my own age, this kind of attention and discussion would make me feel incredibly awkward. Normally, I wouldn't have opted to play an instrument I'd never practiced on, let alone a whole new *type* of instrument, in front of people. Normally I wouldn't choose to perform without accompaniment. But after my long time away from playing regularly, it feels like the old rules have dissolved. There aren't new rules yet, and I get to make—and change—them as I go. I feel like I'm in control this time.

Everyone gets back into the pool, and I float in the middle, looking up at the sky, thinking about how it felt to play Francie's viola. Until I hear Francie ask Sunita what time it is. When Sunita says it's close to three o'clock, both Francie and Ryan curse.

"We should go," Ryan says to Taylor. My guests get out of the pool and wrap themselves in their towels, help Ryan into his chair, and tidy up the pool area. They weave around, tossing their discarded lunch containers and dry clothes into bags, checking around for phones and flip-flops, calling out to each other to make sure no one forgets anything. It's like a chorus of friendship melodies, the orchestration of knowing and caring about each other in these snippets of sound: "Have your shirt?"/ "Where's my hat?" / "This is yours."

The rest of us follow Ryan to the cars, and I'm helping open the door of Ryan's van when I hear the unmistakable sound of another car's wheels on the gravel drive.

It can't be the pool guy. He always comes super early in the mornings, and not usually on a Monday. A few seconds later, my eyes focus and I see a familiar SUV.

My heart and my stomach plummet into a hole in the center of the earth. I have to remind myself to breathe.

"Oh shoot," I say. "That's my mom."

CHAPTER 14

retrograde: when notes are played in reverse
order, starting with the last note and ending
with the beginning note

veryone turns to watch Mom park and get out of
her car. She's wearing a tan suit and high heels that
make her wobble on the gravel. She looks worried,
and tired, and confused. And so angry.

"Rosie," she says, her voice steel blue. "Who—
what is this?" She looks from Mason to Ryan to
Sunita to Taylor to Francie and back to me.

Before I can answer, Mason jumps in. "Hi—
you must be Rosie's mom. I'm Mason. We're"—
he gestures to the group around him—"friends of
Rosie's. From the library. We're all in the improv
class she hangs out in."

Mom stares at him. "And how old are you?"

Mason smiles, though Mom is not charmed. "Sixteen, ma'am. And Ryan is seventeen. We're all—"

"You know Rosie is twelve, right?" Mom asks Mason sharply. I almost want to cover my ears, it hurts so much.

"Mom, they know that," I say. "They're my friends."

"Friends," Mom scoffs. "Yeah, right. Teenagers don't hang out with little kids. They're using you for the pool, I bet." Her eyes take in their towels, our dripping hair and flip-flops.

"No, it's not like that," Sunita says, coming to stand next to Mason. "Rosie is so cool, Mrs., um . . ." She looks at me for help.

"Mrs. Solomon," I say quietly. Mom glares at me, like our surname was a secret I wasn't supposed to tell.

"Yeah, Mrs. Solomon," Mason says. "We all love Rosie. She's so cool and smart, and she—"

I cut him off because I know none of this is making things any better with Mom, and I don't want him to say that I just played music for them. I'm so flustered I don't even get to enjoy the intense wash of pink that spreads through me, from the top of my head down into my feet, because he said the word "love" and he said it about me. I know it's not *that* kind of love. I know he doesn't, and won't ever, feel that way about me. But he said they all love me, and nobody outside my family has ever said that except Julianne.

Mom looks into my eyes for a solid thirty seconds, during which entire oceans of disappointment and disapproval wash over her and crash onto me. Finally she turns back to Mason, who has become the spokesperson of the teens in her eyes.

"It's time for you all to leave," she says. "But first I need contact information for your parents, and a list of your full, legal names."

I have never been so embarrassed or horrified in my life. "Mommm," I whine, like a teen on a TV show whose parents have pulled out baby pictures to show their homecoming date.

"I can text you all the information," Mason volunteers, and Mom tells him her number so he can enter it in his phone. I want to disappear.

"I really don't want to have to involve the authorities," Mom says in an electric, threatening red tone.

"There'll be no need," Sunita says. "Mason will send you everybody's contact info within the hour." She smiles at me, but that only makes me feel worse.

Mom nods, and the five of them scramble into the cars. Mason looks over at me through his driver's side window, trying to convey something, but I can't read it, and I'm so miserable I don't try that hard.

Once the cars have driven off the gravel drive onto the main road, Mom finally speaks again. "What were you thinking?"

I have no words. I don't know where to begin.

Mom opens the passenger door of her car and ushers me in. She drives slowly toward the house.

Suddenly, Mom looks over at me, as if she just realized something. "Wait, are you sure you're okay? Rose, did any of those boys—any of those kids at all—did any of them touch you? Did they make you do anything you didn't feel comfortable doing?"

I think of the feeling of Mason's arm all-too-briefly brushing mine in the water, of his friendly wink. "Mom, I promise, I read that book you gave me about good touches and bad touches, and I remember all the billions of conversations you and I have had about consent, and no one did anything that made me feel the least bit uncomfortable."

Mom sighs with relief. "Thank god," she says, pulling up to the house and stopping the car.

"I've probably been alone in audition rooms with far sketchier people," I say without thinking.

My mom startles, grabbing my shoulder. "Rosie! Has anyone laid a hand—"

"Mom, no! I told you, I heard you on all those conversations we've had about how my body is mine and no one gets to touch it, and power dynamics and grooming and everything you've taught me."

Mom stares at me for a long time again. Eventually she says, "I need some time to process this. And then you and I are going to have a long talk. But for now I need a moment. Go get dressed for dinner. Do not leave the house."

My heart sinks because I was hoping I would get to escape to the shed for a few minutes before dinner. We enter the house in silence, and I wonder what Shanna would say if she were here.

"I can't believe you invited them over here." Mom starts in as soon as she and Grandpa and I are seated at the dinner table. She must've filled Grandpa in at least a little bit about the situation, since he doesn't seem confused, but I can't tell exactly what he does seem to be feeling. Like Mom, he looks exhausted.

"They could've brought drugs. They could've been high or drunk—could've drowned in our pool, and then we would've been responsible! Did you think of that?"

I look down at my plate. "No, Mom, I didn't think of that. But they wouldn't have done something like that. I know them. They're theater kids. They're goofy and funny. I just—"

"You should've asked me first."

"So you could've said no?"

"Yes, so I could've said no and reminded you that it's not normal for teenagers to hang out with children like you."

"Oh," I say, my belly filling up with fiery orange smoke, ready to spew it out into her face. "So now I'm a child. When you want me to play symphonies, I'm mature beyond my years, but now that I have a few friends, I'm a child."

"Rosie," Mom says, her tone a cautioning yellow.

But Grandpa breaks in. "Excuse me," he says. "I realize this is between the two of you, but can we all pause and take a deep breath? What's done is done, nothing bad happened, and let's agree to talk about what to do next time when we're all a little calmer."

"Next time?" Mom practically shrieks, her fork clattering against the plate. "There's no next time."

"Mom!"

"Deep breaths," Grandpa instructs with metal-gray words that settle over us, heavy and final. My orange smoke dissipates in wisps.

After a pause, when it feels safe to speak, I look at each of them in turn. "I'm so incredibly sorry," I say quietly, chains of lavender and gold carefully unspooling from my lips. "I didn't think—"

"*I'll say* you didn't think!" Mom interrupts.

Grandpa gives her a very patient yet stern look. He nods for me to continue.

I say what I practiced in the shower and then again in the mirror while I put on Mom's favorite of my dresses—the light blue one I wore for the competition last fall at the Virginia Festival of Music, when I won first place in the Under-Twenty-Five category.

"I've never been in a situation like that before," I say. "Literally no one ever wants to hang out with me. Let alone multiple people, like this. I didn't know what the rules would even be. So I didn't know I was breaking them."

Mom seems to consider this as if it's new information. As if it never occurred to her that I didn't maliciously and willfully disappoint her.

"And I promise, they're really nice kids."

Vienna saunters over and curls up at my feet in solidarity.

Mom closes her eyes for a second, apparently gathering strength to remain calm. "I know you think that. And I believe you. But you don't know teenagers. I know teenagers."

Grandpa puts a hand on hers and says quietly, "Shoshanna."

"You owe your grandfather an apology," Mom says briskly, looking from him to me.

"I'm so sorry, Grandpa," I say, and I really mean it. "I didn't think about how it's your pool and your property. I didn't consider—"

Grandpa smiles. "It's okay, Rosie. You made a mistake. It happens. Luckily, everything is okay. And we can learn from this."

Now Mom's face is in her hands, and Grandpa gently rubs her back.

"I need a drink," she says.

"Mom," I say mock-seriously, "alcohol is not the way to self-medicate or deal with complicated—"

"Not right now, Rosie," she says, not even looking at me.

Grandpa doesn't try to hide his laughter. "I think our girl is wise beyond her years," he says to Mom.

"That doesn't mean she couldn't fall victim to any number of predatory—"

"I get it, Mom! I promise," I say, joining Grandpa in rubbing circles on her back.

And, for a moment, there is peace at the table.

CHAPTER 15

modulation: a change in key

The chance to play for Grandma Florence comes sooner than I thought it would, but I'm more than ready.

Tuesday morning, during an especially quiet breakfast with Grandpa, Mom comes into the dining room and asks him if he can sit with Grandma Florence until the hospice nurse arrives at ten o'clock. Normally Mom does the morning shifts, but she says she has some errands to run.

At first, I'm disappointed because it means we won't get to swim. But when I register that my grandparents and I will be alone for a while, I realize this is the moment I've been waiting for.

"What are your plans this morning?" Mom asks, looking at me while she feels around in her purse for her car keys. She seems slightly less mad at me than she was yesterday. Her voice is a fairly calm pink.

"I'm just going to read a book," I lie.

She nods, not smiling.

"Mom," I say before she can leave. I stand up from my chair, as if pleading my case in court. "Can you just—can you tell me what you're going to do with all my friends' phone numbers and parents' contact information? I just need to be prepared."

Mom and Grandpa exchange looks, and he nods ever so slightly.

Mom takes in a deep breath and lets it out slowly. "For now," she says, eyes on Grandpa, "nothing."

I feel my body relax, as if I've been holding my breath for years.

"If this truly was an isolated incident, as you say, there is nothing to be done."

"Thank you, Mom. I really, really appreciate—"

"But," she continues, smoothing an invisible wrinkle from her skirt, "I don't think you should hang out with those friends anymore."

A minor chord, an *arpeggio* cascading downward, thunders behind my eyes. "No! Please? Can we at least talk about it some more?"

Mom looks at her phone. "Maybe later, but I've

already given this a lot of thought, and you should be glad I'm not calling their parents, not to mention the police."

"But Mom—"

She turns to leave, as if she can't hear my desperate maroon plea. Maybe she can't—maybe there are tones and notes my mother just can't hear. That would explain why it seems like we speak completely different languages sometimes, my parents and me. It would explain why they barely know me—why they don't trust me, whether it's in my decision to stop playing music or in the friends I choose.

I sink back into my chair, defeated.

"Give it some time," Grandpa says as I take a bite of cold scrambled eggs.

Once I've heard the silver-and-rust-colored starting of Mom's car engine, I remember what I want to ask him. "Can I please play for Grandma while my mom is out?" I whisper, *pianissimo*, even though I know it's not necessary. It's just the three of us in the house, plus Vienna, and she's a great secret keeper.

"Play for her?" Grandpa says, as if prompting me for more information.

"The violin," I say, as if that weren't obvious.

He smiles. "Any particular song?"

I nod. "I think I figured out the song from Hungary."

For a moment, Grandpa looks like he might cry, and then like he might laugh. "Would you like company?" he asks.

I know my answer but don't want to hurt his feelings. "I think I'd like to do this on my own, if that's okay with you?"

Grandpa squeezes my shoulder. "Of course. I know how much this means to you. And to her."

Vienna moseys up behind me as if to say, *But I'll be there, right?*

I reach down and scratch the place between her ears I know she loves. "You can come listen," I whisper to her.

"Hi, Grandma," I say softly as I carry my violin into her room. Vienna springs onto the bed, and Grandma smiles, awake and sitting up.

"Can I play a song for you?" I ask.

"Is it the one from Hungary?" she says eagerly. I take this as an encouraging sign.

I nod, hoping that I'm right. That I've discovered

the melody she's been asking for, possibly a melody she's been yearning to hear for years. But even if it is the right song this time, will she recognize it?

The only way to find out is to play.

Vienna tucks her chin on Grandma's lap, and I tuck mine onto my violin, leaning into it like it's a trusted old friend. I actually miss the bigger, heftier feel of Francie's viola, the deeper tones and richer sound of it. But for this performance, the familiarity of my violin feels right.

I breathe in, the way a conductor does to let an orchestra know they're about to drop the baton for the opening notes. And I play the pictures from that album.

I play in blacks and whites, and in all the gray shades in between. I play every color of the spectrum in its time, turning the images from achromatic to technicolor with each note. Pigmentation and sound gradually build to fill the room.

If I use Grandpa's definition, I'm traveling through time as I play, because I'm here, with my feet on the creaky wooden floor of my grandparents' house, in the dim light of the lamps perched on matching wooden tables on either side of the bed. But I'm also with Dahlia, marching proudly through the streets of Munkacs, unafraid to be herself, to play her music out loud, before she knew how much danger she was in. I'm following her as we play in tandem, and then in harmony, and then in cascading rounds.

I feel the presence of all the generations between us, but I could reach out and touch her if I wanted to. She's so close to me, I can hear every single shade of gray in her skin, her hair, her clothing.

I'm with Shanna, humming the notes subconsciously, because the music flows through our blood like a code. The notes have existed in my DNA all along, but hearing Shanna's unknowing cues was what first unlocked them for me.

The song from Hungary is sad and joyous and loud and quiet and fast and slow. It is black and white and every single color that the human ear can hear.

I play with the kind of joy and feeling that Dr. Sascha always talked about when she said it wasn't enough to simply get the notes right. I never knew how to access that kind of energy until this moment. Despite all the contests I've won and all the awards and accolades, I never actually played music this well until now. Never gave the music the undertones and dimensions that come with the stories behind the notes. For all the colors I saw, I never infused them into my performances—I kept so much inside. I kept so much color to myself because I was scared of being too much.

Don't tell anyone you can play whole symphonies in your head.

Don't tell anyone you can see music as colors.

Don't tell anyone you can hear colors as music.

Don't tell anyone you're Jewish.

Don't let anyone see you.

Don't let anyone hear you.

How many generations of us have hidden something? And how many of us have hidden the *same* things? Will the truth be a secret forever, or a surprise? We hide our gifts because we're scared of standing out in the wrong ways. And when we share them, we do it in a way that's socially acceptable and comfortable for others. The full truth has always been a secret, instead of a surprise.

By learning the song, I've broken the code. By playing the song, I break the silence. I'm finished hiding, and I'm done playing in a way that makes everyone else comfortable. Whatever perceived or real dangers are out there, I'm not scared.

And that's how I know it's time to end the song. I finish with a flourish of the bow and just the right amount of vibrato. The room glows gray—all the grays—and that final note hangs suspended, a soft piece of cloud. As long as that fragment remains, Dahlia and Shanna are in the room with us. As the note fades and the cloud dissipates, it becomes, once again, just Grandma Florence and me, and Vienna.

I might've played for hours—I really have no idea. When the final cloud is gone, Grandma closes her eyes. I'm scared to ask, even though I felt the answer from the moment I played that first note.

"Was that the song?" I whisper.

The woman who can barely speak, who can hardly hear, who can rarely remember, nods. She smiles.

She says, "That was the song from Hungary. The one my mother used to sing to me. The one I sang to my daughters. The one I hoped you knew."

A tear runs down my cheek and I wipe it away with my hand. I'm not sure exactly what, but I know that Grandma Florence is telling me so much more than just the content of her words. It's like a recipe, and I want to take in every single ingredient.

"I know it now," I tell her. Setting the violin on an armchair, I move closer to the bed, the side Vienna's not on, so that I can sit next to Grandma Florence and take her hand.

"Not everyone can hear the song," she says. "And those who can—many can't remember it."

"I'll remember it."

"Yes, you will."

More tears escape. It's time to say goodbye for now. I lean down over my grandmother's delicate, beautiful face and kiss her cheeks. "Thank you for the song," I say.

"Thank *you* for the song," she says. She doesn't call me Rosie, because I am so many names right now, so much more than myself alone. I am all of them, and she knows that.

I sit with her until her breathing is steady and I'm certain she's asleep.

"You have to take music lessons," I tell Shanna. It only took me a few minutes to put the violin back in Mom's room and find my way to the shed, to her, to the sunshine on the floor and the brown hum of the wooden walls.

Shanna looks at me, surprised. "But I told you, I can't—"

"You *have to*," I tell her.

Now that I've finally connected the dots—me, my mother, Florence, Dahlia—into the continuous circle of time and family, I have this sense that I can change things: in Shanna's time, in mine. It's as if a portal has opened since I played the song from Hungary. A thread exists between Shanna and me, and I can almost see it, shimmering in the skylight's glow.

I know there will be consequences, if this works. I might change the entire course of Shanna's life, and threaten the existence of mine. But that's a chance I have to take.

"What is this about?" Shanna asks.

"I heard you humming the other day. You have a beautiful voice, and you know all the notes."

"What do you mean, I know all the notes?"

"To the song!" I know I sound confused and lost, but this is the clearest I have ever felt.

"What song?"

I shake my head, trying to wipe away all the unnecessary noise and colors. "It doesn't matter—you'll understand it later."

"But I told you, I have to do my bat mitzvah. There isn't time or money for anything else." She's impatient with me, dismissive, but I cut her off.

"You have to figure out how to have both. This

is your life, and I know it sounds strange, but I think you *have* to play the violin. You have to learn. I think you have a gift."

"Rosie! Stop it. What are you even saying?" Shanna looks upset, like I'm scaring her.

Good! Maybe she needs to be shaken up a little, enough that she'll make a change before it's too late.

Shanna puts a hand on my arm. "Why are you trying to force me to do the exact thing you wish your parents wouldn't force you to do?"

That silences all the color for a second.

"Someday," I tell her, looking into her eyes, "you're going to have a daughter, and if you don't fix this, it will ruin everything between you and her."

Shanna looks terrified now. "*What?*"

I tug my hair out of its ponytail, looking for relief from the force that's building inside me. "If you don't play, then you'll want *her* to, and the balance will be off. You have to take some of the music, so it isn't all on her. Because it's too much for her to carry on her own."

"My parents won't let me," Shanna starts, timid and quiet, but trying to meet me in some part of the conversation she understands. "My mom doesn't like music . . ."

"That's not true. She only thinks she doesn't, because she thinks it's dangerous to stand out like *her* mother did. But she does like music. It lives in her. And the spells she has? I think they happen because she isn't letting the music *out*." I'm trying to put into words all the crystal-clear things I saw and heard when I was playing the song for Grandma Florence, but now, in the shed, I suspect none of it is making sense. "I think she needs this. *You* need this. You have to have the music in your life, and you need a way to let it out."

Shanna has gone pale. "Rosie, you're kind of freaking me out," she whispers.

"I know," I say, grabbing her hand. "I'm kind of freaking myself out, honestly. But I have to say this, and you have to hear it."

Shanna shakes her head. "Hear what?"

I take her other hand, so that we're facing each other like mirror images. "Do you hear colors, Shanna? Or see music?"

Her face is blank.

"You can tell me. Please tell me. I know you do. Just say it."

Tears begin to fall from Shanna's eyes, and I know I've gone too far. "I'm sorry," she says. "I don't know—I can't."

"It's okay, Shanna—"

She pulls away, wrenching her hands from mine. "I have to go," she cries, and for the first time, I see Shanna leave the shed first.

♪

The last time someone ran from me crying like that, it was Julianne, after our big fight.

I've tried for months not to think about that day, about all the things we said to each other, but now I can't avoid it. It's a song stuck in my head, playing on a loop in the background all the time.

I was supposed to sleep over at Julianne's house one Friday night in April. Her birthday was coming up that following Monday, so her mom said she could have me sleep over in celebration, before they left to visit Julianne's aunt and uncle in New Jersey for the rest of the weekend.

Honestly, I was dreading the sleepover. I'd spent the previous week working on a particularly tricky passage in a Mendelssohn violin concerto, staying up long after my parents had gone to bed, sleeping only a few hours each night. And I still didn't feel like I'd mastered it. The concert was only a few weeks away and I wanted to feel certain I could nail it, backward, forward, upside down and in my sleep. I wasn't in the mood to stay up late with Julianne, talking about her crushes on popular girls who didn't know she existed, my lack of crushes on anyone because I didn't have time for crushes, or how hard the science test was at school. I didn't want to watch a movie about teenagers doing things I'd never do, like sneak out or go to parties and get drunk or fall in love. I just wanted to squeeze in three extra hours of violin practice and go to bed by nine o'clock.

So, the day before the scheduled sleepover, when we were walking together after school, I asked Julianne if we could reschedule.

"I'm just so tired," I told her as we cut across the quad. "I think I'd have more fun if we could do it next weekend instead."

The sun glinted in Julianne's shiny red hair, the freckles on her face dancing in the light like *pizzicato* notes. "You're joking, right?" she said, staring straight ahead.

I scowled. "No. Why would I joke?"

Julianne turned and looked at me, her green eyes flashing with anger. "Rosie! You know how important this is to me!"

I was confused—we'd had other sleepovers. Sometimes, if Mom had to go somewhere, like to see my grandparents for the weekend, and Dad was working on a Friday, I'd stay at Julianne's. Usually I'd arrive late, after a symphony rehearsal or a performance, and leave early the next morning for a competition or audition, but Julianne always understood.

Or I thought she did.

But that day, she paused in the middle of the quad, the green of her eyes in perfect thirds above the grass below, and the glare of the sun hitting the fifth, creating a chord so achingly beautiful I had a hard time processing what Julianne was even saying at first.

"It's my birthday!" she wailed, and she actually stomped her foot for emphasis, like a child trying to play the drums, thinking there was no musical craft to it, just force.

"I know," I said, looking around, hoping no one we knew was watching us as Julianne made a scene. "Look," I said, pulling her over to a more secluded area with a bench, in the shade of a huge tree. "Birthdays are just days. It's not the date that matters. We can celebrate all the same next weekend!"

I was trying to channel Mom, who'd said this to

me any number of times over the years when I had to perform or audition or rehearse on my birthday.

Julianne stared at me, her mouth wide open. "Rosie, we've been talking about this sleepover for a month. We planned way in advance and made sure you had no other obligations!"

I blinked, trying to remember these details, but all I could really think about was my rehearsal schedule for the Mendelssohn concerto. I wracked my brain as to why we had that weekend off. Oh, right, I remembered—Dr. Sascha was at a conference, and the conductor of the orchestra where I'd be guest-playing the Mendelssohn was at the same conference. But they probably expected the musicians to spend any extra time working on our parts, like I'd been doing.

Julianne looked at me expectantly.

I cringed. "I'm sorry. Can you repeat whatever you just—"

Julianne slumped onto the bench with a growl. I had never heard her make a noise like that—deep plums and aubergine hues reverberating around us in circles like a stormy sky. Usually Julianne is so composed, so prim and quiet.

"I said I was sorry," I started, but Julianne is like

a percussion instrument that can't be tamped. Once you strike it and the sound begins, you just have to let the vibrations go until they cease naturally. I sat on the bench with her, ready to ride out her tantrum.

"It's always something with you! You're just soooo busy, and everything you do is soooo important."

To my surprise, I saw tears in her eyes.

"It's like nothing matters to you besides your violin," she continued. "We've been friends for five years, and I can count on one hand the number of times you *haven't* had to cancel or reschedule plans, or show up late because of a concert or leave early for a rehearsal."

I recoiled. "Well, yeah, I mean . . ." I tried to think of words to match hers, to absorb her flow of icy silver in a warmer tone of red or pink. "I played the violin before I knew you, so it's not like you didn't know this was a thing with me."

Julianne was crying in earnest now, loudly and sloppily, grabbing a tissue from the pocket of her backpack. "I knew it was *a* thing. I just didn't realize it was going to be *the only* thing."

"What's that supposed to mean?" My voice rose to a burning orange, losing all its calming warmth and edging toward fiery flames.

"You're never there when I need you, Rosie!" she cried. "Heck, you're never even there when I just *want* you to be. What kind of friend are you?"

The flames inside me crackled, lightning strikes in a rising storm. "I'm the kind of friend who has a life! Unlike some people who only go to school and then just sit at home the rest of the time and, I don't know, read The Garden of Fairy books and watch reality TV."

As soon as I said it, I knew I'd gone too far. I'd repeated something Mom had said about Julianne and the other kids at my school, even though when Mom said it I'd thought it sounded unfair—cruel. Truthfully, I was jealous of Julianne and the other kids who got to obsess over books and watch TV.

There was a long, long pause. A *fermata*, on repeat.

"Well, I'm sorry we can't all be prodigies," Julianne said quietly.

"Come on, Julianne," I started. "I'm sorry, but—"

"My mom says that your violin career is unhealthy, and that someday you're going to look back on all the normal kid stuff you've missed and regret it."

That stunned me into silence.

"My mom also thinks I shouldn't be your friend anymore. She says I deserve better. I deserve a friend who is *there*. I deserve a friend to take a pottery class with me after school or to go to drama camp with me this summer. I deserve someone who has time for me."

I held out my hands to the sides, palms up. "I said I was sorry!"

Julianne didn't look angry anymore. She just looked exhausted. "It's not your fault, Rosie. I probably should've said something after you didn't show up for my dad's funeral. And I've been making excuses for you ever since. But I think . . . I think I'm done."

I didn't move. I didn't dare breathe.

"You don't want to be friends anymore?" I whispered, like a thin piece of yellow tissue paper, so pale and see-through it was almost white.

Julianne smiled sadly and stood up to walk away. "I don't think we ever were. Not the real kind."

Now that I've driven Shanna away too, I can't help wondering if I'll ever figure out how to be a real friend to anyone.

CHAPTER 16

lament: music written and played for the
purpose of mourning the dead or for moments
of loss or separation

I know it's happened even before I hear the words.
I see it on my mother's face as soon as I wake up.
She's sitting on the edge of my bed, with tears in her
eyes, and she hugs me so tightly.

"Grandma Florence died," she says. "It was
peaceful—in her sleep, sometime last night. Your
dad is on his way. The funeral is tomorrow."

I blink in confusion. "Tomorrow? But . . ."

"I know, it's fast. But that's how Jewish funerals
are. We bury the dead within twenty-four hours.
We're fudging it a little to give your aunt Lily time
to get here, but we have to do it as soon as possible."

I sit up straighter. I look at her. My mom, but

also Shanna. "Are you okay?" I ask.

She shakes her head and begins to sob. "I'm not, but I will be," she says, more to herself than to me.

I put my arms around her, and she leans into me. I let her cry for as long as she wants to. I look for that thread of connection between us that I saw between Shanna and me in the shed. But grief sits cloudy all around us, black and red and gray. Everything else in the world is suspended; this is just a time to grieve together. I feel as though I hardly knew Grandma Florence, and yet through Shanna and Dahlia and the song from Hungary, I also know her better than almost anyone else in my life.

"Mom," I say gently, once she's dried some of her tears and the relentless tempo of her cries have slowed to a broad, solemn *largo*, "what happens now?"

It turns out that Judaism prescribes exactly what happens after a person dies, and I'm so grateful for that. It's like we have sheet music—a symphony, really— with each of our parts written out so that when we all play them, the sad harmonies intertwine exactly as they're supposed to.

Mom and Grandpa will have to pick out a casket, but that's mostly a formality, Mom tells me, since Jews are usually buried in simple pine coffins, wearing white cotton garments. Grandma's body has already been taken to the funeral home, where a designated person, called a shomeret, will sit with her body until she's buried.

"To keep her company?" I ask Mom timidly when she mentions this. I like the idea that Grandma Florence isn't alone.

Mom smiles, tugging on a black silk shirt. I'm in her room with her, watching her get dressed, preparing for this thing I know she's dreaded her whole life—even if she's had weird ways of showing it for as long as I can remember.

"Jewish tradition states that a part of the soul remains in the body until burial. So the shomeret is there to comfort her while she's . . ." Mom trails off, as if searching for the word.

"In limbo?" I ask. It makes me think of an unresolved chord in music, waiting for the dissonance to resolve into the tonic.

She smiles sadly. "Yes. Limbo is a good way to describe it. Unfinished business."

I think about the song from Hungary that I

finally played for Grandma Florence yesterday. It feels like Grandma Florence has been in limbo for years, her memories trapped in her body. Maybe now she's actually no longer in limbo. I'm glad she got to hear the song one last time. Maybe she was waiting for that.

But I don't say any of this to Mom. I'm not ready to tell her I played the violin for Grandma Florence.

When Mom and Grandpa leave to choose the casket, I'm alone in the house for the first time ever.

I'm not sure what to do. I'm not allowed to go back to the library, ever since the pool incident, but I wouldn't want to anyway. I don't want to go to the shed. I can't go swim alone. I don't have anyone to play the violin for. Now it feels like I'm the one in limbo.

I haven't cried since Mom told me that Grandma died. I know I'm sad, but all I feel is numb.

I hear the front door open and am flooded with relief to not be by myself anymore.

"Dad!" I shout as I run to the foyer.

He puts down his suitcase and hugs me tightly. Debussy's "Violin Sonata" floods my head. I'm not sure what to say. There aren't any words that could mean enough to say out loud right now. Only music.

And since I don't have a way to share the music coursing through me, I just hold my father tight.

"How many surgeries did you have to postpone to come here?" I ask, once we've drawn apart and he's following me into the living room.

"None," he says. "The other doctors offered to cover for me, and everyone will be okay."

"Oh. Good!"

Dad often acts like he's the only person who can help his patients. Hearing him say his colleagues can fill in is new. I know he's needed at the hospital, but he's needed here too, and I'm so glad to have him.

"Your aunt Lily's flight gets in this evening," he adds, "so she'll be here late tonight."

I'd almost forgotten about Aunt Lily, to be honest. But now that Dad's brought her up, I can't wait to see her. After hearing Shanna talk about their childhood, and after discovering our family's history, I feel as if she's another missing movement in the symphony I've been piecing together this summer.

We're already done with dinner by the time Aunt Lily texts Mom from the airport. Her plane's just landed and she still has to get a cab to bring her here. I'm a little worried that I'll get sent to bed before she shows up.

But just before ten o'clock, we hear the cab pull into the driveway. Mom jumps up to open the front door, and Aunt Lily strides in, rolling a small suitcase in one hand and carrying something unmistakably instrument-shaped in the other.

Mom lets out a wordless, joyful, magenta exclamation. I watch in wonder as she and her sister embrace, tears streaming down both their faces. I don't think I've ever seen Mom this emotional.

Aunt Lily wears a flowy cape-like top covered in a patchwork of different prints and colors, like a jumbled collection of folk songs in languages I don't speak. She smells like a field of wildflowers. Her hair, curly and wild like mine and Mom's, flows down to the middle of her back. Vienna greets her like an old friend, and Aunt Lily holds the dog's face in her hands and kisses Vienna's nose in greeting. She hugs Dad. She holds Grandpa tight for a full minute as more tears come from both of them. Finally, it's my turn.

"Golden Rose," she says, as if we're somehow both meeting for the first time and the oldest of friends. "You don't have to hug me. I know it's been a long time."

But her arms are outstretched and I gravitate to

her embrace the same way I'm drawn to the shed.

I close my eyes while I hug Aunt Lily, yet I see so many colors and images. Flowers and cobblestone streets and sunsets and dresses. She's full of music I don't recognize, but I immediately like it.

"I have something for you," Lily says to me as we all walk into the living room together. Vienna stays right by my side.

"For me?" I ask tentatively. Of course I noticed the instrument case she carried in, and of course I'm curious about it, but . . .

Mom breaks in. "No, Lily. Didn't I tell you that Rosie's not playing? Don't bring it up now."

I do a double take. It figures that the one time Mom actually tries to respect my wishes I don't actually need her to.

"I'd like to know more," I say, looking from one sister to the other.

Mom looks skeptical, but Lily smiles and pats the sofa next to her for me to sit down. She picks up the instrument case and sets it between us. It's shaped differently than my violin case, but maybe that's because it's Austrian and old. "This belonged to your great-grandmother Dahlia, Grandma Florence's mother."

She flicks the briefest glance toward my parents, who both look like they're braced for some kind of disaster.

"I don't know how much you know about this," Lily says to me. "But Dahlia and her family lived in Hungary until the Holocaust. They were taken to concentration camps, and most of them . . . didn't make it. Even the ones who survived never came back to their homes."

I nod, staying quiet, unsure how much I should admit to already knowing.

Lily goes on, her rich maroon voice cutting through the cold, silent blue of the room. "Some neighbors kept the family's most precious things hidden and safe from the Germans. They held on to these things for years, long after the war was over, thinking perhaps Dahlia or her parents would come back. I had hoped something like this had happened. When I first went to Europe years ago, it was partly to look for clues about our family—objects, records, anything. It took a lot of research and time, but I eventually located their belongings." She pats the instrument case. "I've been holding on to this in case you might like to have it someday. In case you might like to play it."

"She won't want it," Mom says again, but Grandpa shushes her, a bronze stream of soothing light.

I can barely breathe, I want to open the case so badly. But I know that if I touch Dahlia's violin, I'll need to play it, and I'm not ready to play in front of my parents yet. I need the music to be all mine for a little while longer.

As if she can read my mind, Lily says briskly, "It's late. Maybe I should hang on to this for now, and we can look at it together tomorrow."

"I'd like that," I whisper, just barely able to eke out a green tone of gratitude.

Suddenly everyone springs to life. Vienna needs to go outside, my parents both say how tired they are, and Grandpa offers Lily some dinner.

"I don't even know what time of day it is," Lily says, scratching Vienna behind the ears. The grown-ups scatter to the kitchen and the bedrooms while I let the dog out. By the time Vienna and I come back inside, no one else is around. But Lily has left the instrument in its case right there on the sofa.

As if for me to take it.

I gently pick up the case and carry it upstairs as Vienna trails me, keeping guard. Whether she's guarding me or the violin, I don't know.

I hug the instrument case to my chest as we tip-toe down the hall, until we get to the closed door of what was Grandma Florence's room.

"I think this is where I want to play it," I say to Vienna, even though I know she doesn't understand my words.

The room looks pretty much the same, except that the bed is neatly made with fresh linens and the hospital equipment has been taken away already. Vienna climbs up onto the bed like she used to when Grandma Florence was in it, and I carefully unlock the case.

In all the excitement of Aunt Lily's arrival, I didn't fully register the shape of the case until now. But as soon as I see the instrument inside, I realize it's not a violin at all. The wider body and the longer neck, the thicker strings—it's a viola.

I take the bow from the case and tighten it quickly. I pluck the thick, wire-wrapped strings and tune them, the top string an A instead of the violin's E. I can tell that the strings were replaced somewhat recently and have been regularly tuned—that someone has taken care of this instrument over the years. It's in remarkably good condition.

Like Francie's viola, this feels both familiar and thrillingly new. But unlike Francie's, this instrument was made for me. Every inch of it feels like it was built with my body in mind. With Dahlia's body in mind, maybe. So maybe it was, in a way, made for me.

I'm not ready to play Grandma's song again, the song from Hungary. I think it will be a while until I can. So instead, I decide to play something new, some folk music I heard when I hugged Aunt Lily. The viola's sound is mellow and deep, mournful but full of hope. It has history and depth and colors I've never seen before. It feels like home and sounds like the whole world in one place.

I stop playing because I feel someone watching me. When I turn, Aunt Lily is standing in the doorway.

"Yes," she says when our eyes meet. "This is perfect."

"Thank you," I say, as if any words could express how grateful I am for this gift she's saved for me.

She nods, and there's a silent understanding between us. She won't tell anyone else I've played it yet—not until I'm ready. And I will take good care of the viola. After all, it was always meant to be mine.

CHAPTER 17

agitato: in an agitated manner; used as a direction in music

The funeral goes by in a blur. The synagogue is full of people I don't know: older ladies and men stooped with age, neighbors who've brought along photos and food and memories to share. The service is mostly in English, though the rabbi and the cantor pray in Hebrew. Even though I don't know the language, I feel its music deep in my bones, as if it's always been part of me. The room is full of tiny pixels of color, snippets of sounds, fragments of memory and ancient traditions.

But it's at the burial that I feel the most. Six of us go to the cemetery behind the synagogue: Grandpa and Lily, my parents and me, and the rabbi. Someone has already dug the grave and lined the area around it with green fabric. There's a wooden slab for us to walk on as we follow the rabbi to the folding chairs set up at one end.

I haven't cried since I found out Grandma Florence died. I wish I could. I watch Grandpa and Aunt Lily weep openly, and Dad sheds a few quiet tears, but Mom and I are equally dry-eyed. I wonder if she feels numb, like I do.

The rabbi chants more prayers in Hebrew, but I can barely hear them over the swell of music in my mind—a grand symphony of the varying shades of green, from the bright kelly-green fabric lining the grave to the hillside covered in late-summer grass to the pale, fragile sage of withering bushes already preparing for autumn. This symphony is a variation on a theme, and, of course, the theme is the song from Hungary. It's what I would play out here if I were alone, if the song and the moment could be all mine. I would play the song in this green key, and then transpose to something blue, then a purple key, and so on, until I'd played grief in every iteration the ear can hear. It would take all day—maybe even multiple days.

Mom has prepared me for most of the Jewish funeral rituals. Like how, before the service started, we were given ribbons to pin on our clothes, which the rabbi then tore—*keriah* in Hebrew—to symbolize the tearing of the fabric of our family, physical evidence of our grief. Mom explained shiva, the seven-day mourning period. She told me how someone is at the house now, covering all our mirrors with black cloth so we're not tempted to think of frivolous things like how we look during this time of intense sadness.

But I guess Mom forgot to tell me about the burial itself. Two men from the funeral home use a pulley system to lower the plain pine box—adorned only with a wooden Jewish star on the top—into the ground. I hear Aunt Lily gasp with the finality of it. Grandpa holds her tight, and I can see that she and Mom squeeze each other's hands. The rabbi recites a prayer called the Mourner's Kaddish.

And now comes a part I wasn't expecting: he takes a shovelful of dirt and tosses it deep into the grave, where it lands with a jolting *thwack* on the wood of the casket.

The rabbi places the shovel back in the graveside pile of dirt and motions to Grandpa. Grandpa picks up the shovel and uses the back of it to collect some dirt from the pile.

"What's he doing?" I whisper to Mom.

Mom doesn't whisper. "We each contribute dirt to fill the grave. It's a mitzvah—a good deed. It's how we show we're all in this together."

The rabbi explains, "Your grandfather used the back of the shovel to show how hard it is to do this—how burying your grandmother is something we wish we didn't have to do, something we do reluctantly."

I nod as Grandpa pushes his scoop of dirt into the grave with a charcoal-colored chord of devastation.

"And we don't hand the shovel to each other," the rabbi adds. "We each put it back on the ground for the next person to take. Another way to show it's hard, and that in spite of that, we're doing it of our own will."

I watch Aunt Lily, then Dad, and then Mom each shovel in a clump of dirt that lands with a distinct sound on the coffin. The tone and timbre change every time because there's more dirt collecting on the surface.

I'm the last one to pick up the shovel. It's tough to accumulate dirt on the back side of the shovel, but I manage. The smattering of dirt lands in a perfect *arpeggio*, the first major chord I've heard all day.

It's time to leave, to let the professionals from the funeral home finish the burial and plant the seeds of the grass that will grow over Grandma's grave. In keeping with Jewish tradition, we won't add a head-stone until exactly a year from now, when we'll all come back to unveil it. That way, we'll continue to gather, and to remember Grandma Florence. I like that tradition, the promise of more times together.

Aunt Lily stands at the edge of the grave crying loudly, and Mom puts her arms around her sister.

"I don't want to leave her here," Lily sobs into Mom's shoulder. "I don't want her to be alone."

Grandpa takes one of Lily's hands in one of his and one of Mom's in the other.

"We have to," he says. "We are still alive. We have to walk away. It's what your mother would want. She would want us to go and continue living."

I think of how, in all the years that Grandma Florence has been in failing health—moving less and less, talking less and less, remembering less and less—Grandpa has kept living. He had to. He made sandwiches and swam in the pool and read the news-paper and walked the dog. We are still alive, so we have to go on.

Grandpa grasps his daughters' hands as he looks

toward the coffin. "I said goodbye to you a long time ago, my love," he murmurs. "And yet, you'll never really be gone so long as we remember." He takes and exhales a deep breath, and the three of them walk toward the synagogue, where fancy black cars wait to take us home.

♪

Per Jewish tradition, we're going to sit shiva for seven days.

Neighbors I've never met and friends of my grandparents I didn't know existed pour into the house on the first day, their voices a steady hum of divergent and dissonant notes. They bring casseroles and cakes, and Mom and Aunt Lily spend hours talking to old friends they haven't seen in years. Grandpa is always surrounded by people who make sure he has everything he needs. Dad has become the food director, deciding what to freeze, what to serve, and what to store in the neighbor's refrigerator for the next day. Even though Tamar's here, Dad insists that she shouldn't have to work during this time. He always seems to be in the middle of planning or storing or defrosting something.

I've never been among so many people at once and yet so utterly alone. I've played the violin for much larger crowds, of course, but I try to avoid being *in* them. They make me feel overstimulated and overwhelmed. I get a headache within hours. It makes me think of Grandma Florence's spells. I wonder if she got headaches like mine from seeing sound everywhere.

As the days pass, I sometimes go upstairs in my room to read, but usually one of my parents finds me after an hour or so and asks me to come downstairs and "talk to our guests." I feel like I used to when I played the violin—like a performing circus animal on display. Everyone asks me questions about school (feels like a lifetime ago), friends (I literally don't have any), or violin (oh, look over there at that casserole!) and I mostly try to avoid getting into conversations whenever possible.

I long to go down to the shed, but I also dread it. The last time I was there, when I told Shanna she needed to play the violin, she looked at me like she didn't want to see me again anytime soon. I don't want to ambush her if she still needs space. Or risk that she won't show up at all.

I can't go swimming either. Mom says it wouldn't

be appropriate while everyone is at the house for shiva. Dahlia's viola is waiting to be played, but I know that wouldn't be appropriate now either.

I'm lonely in the worst kind of way, except for Vienna, who stays by my side as if she's protecting me from everyone who comes in the house. If it weren't for her, I think I would've exploded by now.

On the afternoon of the fifth day of shiva, Mom finds me hiding in the sunroom, petting Vienna on the couch.

Her face looks different. She's smiling, a kind of smile I haven't seen on her all summer. Or maybe since before I stopped playing the violin. "Rosie? Can you come with me?"

I look behind me, as if there might be another person, let alone another Rosie, there. "What for?" I ask, full of thin mustard-colored waves of trepidation.

She just motions for me to follow her, so I do. We go through the almost-empty living room and the crowded dining room—Dad has just put out a fresh quiche and the ladies from the Temple Sisterhood group are there to eat it.

When we get to the foyer by the front door, Mom turns to me, blocking whatever's behind her.

"There's someone here to see you." When she steps aside I see Julianne.

The room is awash in the steady hum of blue shiva noise, with a pastel pink haze around Julianne as she says, "Rosie. Hi. I'm really sorry for your loss."

For the first time since Grandma Florence died, my eyes fill with tears.

I'm scared to take a step closer, in case she turns out to be a figment of my imagination, the same fear I've had about Shanna in the shed. Luckily, Julianne bridges the gap between us. Before I can process what's going on, her bony arms are around my shoulders and I am hugging her so hard.

"What are you doing here?" I ask, wiping at my eyes with my sleeve once we let each other go. I haven't seen her outside of school since our fight.

Julianne smiles and glances to her left, where I see her mom standing awkwardly by the door, her purse in her hand, a cotton sweater looped over her shoulders despite the one-hundred-degree weather.

Mom ushers Mrs. Farnsworth toward the buffet in the dining room, their swirls of yellow-sounding pleasantries mixing into the hum of blue. We're still in the crush of shiva visitors making their ways from the table into the living room. I want to take Julianne somewhere we can have a conversation.

"Want to go outside and talk?" I ask her. Julianne nods, smiling slightly like she does when she sees a girl she has a crush on or does well on a test.

It's a shock to transition from the indoor air conditioning to the heat and humidity outside. I guide Julianne around the side of the house to the back terrace.

"This is so pretty," Julianne says, observing the view. She's wearing the bracelet her dad gave her in second grade. Seeing it makes my tears well all over again.

I sit on the edge of the stone wall and gesture for her to join me. "So, are you finally going to tell me what you're doing here?"

Julianne sits, her long red hair tickling my arm slightly. "Your mom called mine and told her about your grandmother. She thought maybe I'd want to send you a letter or call you on the phone."

A tear streaks down my cheek and I don't bother to wipe it away. "But you came here?"

Julianne nods. "I remember what it's like."

My tears come faster, and a sob escapes. Julianne takes a little package of tissues out of the pocket of her navy dress and hands me one. I love that about her. She's always prepared.

"But . . ." I wipe my nose. "But I didn't even come to your dad's funeral. And yet, you came all the way up here? It's, like, a five-hour drive!"

Julianne puts an arm around my shoulders and hands me another tissue. She seems so much older than when I last saw her, and I wonder if I do too. She still smells like honeysuckle and cookies, and there's something so comforting about it.

"I'm sorry about our fight," I say. "And I'm sorry I didn't come to your dad's funeral last summer. And I'm sorry—"

"It's okay," she says, interrupting me before I can apologize for a thousand other mistakes.

"I had no idea how it felt to lose someone. When your dad died, I barely understood. I didn't have any real sense of how you must've felt. And it didn't even occur to me that I could leave camp to be there for you."

Julianne shifts so she's facing me, and I do the same. I'm close enough to see her freckles, multiplied by the summer sunshine. "Rosie, it's okay. I never truly held that against you. I was just saying something my mom had said, honestly."

"I know," I say, another sob escaping, "but that's just one of a thousand times I wasn't there for you. I was so wrapped up in my music, and I didn't realize . . . I let you down so much. I didn't think I'd get another chance. But you're here."

"Of course I'm here," she says, a tear escaping from her eyes too. "I begged my mom to drive me up here. I didn't want you to be alone."

"Thank you," I whisper.

"And I think I owe you an apology too," she adds after a moment.

I'm shocked. "For what?" I can't imagine what she has to be sorry for. I'm the one who never put our friendship first.

She shrugs. "I think maybe I was being a little selfish. My mom and I talked about it in the car."

I blink steadily, breathing in purple rhythms of hopeful *arpeggios*.

Julianne goes on. "I know that it's not like you *choose* to be busy all the time. That's not your fault. I shouldn't have blamed you."

There's so much behind those words—a harmony underscoring the melody, like a secret code. She knows that so much of my life hasn't been my choice. So much of it is my mother's. I've never felt able to say that to Julianne. Complaining always felt disloyal to Mom, or ungrateful. But knowing that Julianne gets it is such a relief.

I look out at the tree line, where the sun is starting to sink. "Well, even if you understand, you can still be annoyed that I'm not available when you need me, or when you just want to hang out."

Out of the corner of my eye I see Julianne nod. "I think I've realized," she says, just above a whisper, "that even though you'll always be my best friend, I can't let you be my only friend anymore."

I turn to her, her face bathed in the orange sunlight. "I'm still your best friend?" I'm crying again.

Julianne is crying too. "I hope so. I know I said our friendship was over, but I shouldn't have. I'm sorry. I'd like to be best friends again. As long as it's okay if I have other friends. Maybe even another best friend, in a different way."

I nod, thinking of Mason and Ryan and Sunita and Francie and Taylor. Of how well they all seemed to click, without any pair excluding or competing with the others. Of everything they meant to me this summer, even though I never got to know them well or truly be part of their group. I think of Grandpa taking me swimming and Aunt Lily giving me the viola. The many kinds of friendships someone can have. All the people you need in your life to build a satisfying, full symphony.

"I can definitely work with that," I say, using one of Julianne's tissues to wipe my eyes. "And I promise things are going to be different from here on out. I'm going to be different."

She gives me another hug. "I'm here, whatever you want to be."

CHAPTER 18

fermata: stop; a rest or a note held for a length
of time chosen by the performer or conductor

After Julianne and her mom leave to drive to New Jersey to see her cousins, the shiva crowd thins to just a few people from the synagogue. They always make sure there are at least ten adults—a minyan, or the minimum number of practicing Jews needed for a prayer service. I don't count, since I haven't had a bat mitzvah and I'm not considered an adult in the Jewish community. The rabbi comes at six o'clock to recite the brief evening shiva prayers, but I can barely pay attention. All I can think about is my talk with Julianne.

After the final guests leave, Aunt Lily goes to her room, Dad goes for a run, and Grandpa goes to the sunroom to catch up on his newspapers. There's a pile almost as tall as the couch of ones he hasn't read in the past several days, but he doesn't seem bothered.

Tamar is gone, Mom and I are alone in the kitchen.

"Thank you for calling Julianne's mom," I say quietly, not sure if I want to have this conversation with her but unable to keep from saying something.

Mom smiles. She looks even more tired than she did earlier in the week. I wish I could tell her to take a whole day off, but I know that isn't possible.

"I didn't think they'd drive all the way up here," she says with a small laugh. "Especially not after the way we all left things in the spring."

She sits at the kitchen table, and I sink down in the chair across from her. My legs are exhausted and my shoe straps have been rubbing a blisters into my left heel. I don't know how to put into words what I want to say to her. It's like a melody I can't grasp, just beyond the edges of my mind. Like a texture from a dream I can't transpose into wakeful music.

"Mom, I think I want to have a bat mitzvah." That's definitely not where I originally thought this conversation was going. The words just flew out of my mouth.

Mom raises her eyebrows. "Okaaaaay," she says,

drawing the word out. I can't tell if she's getting mad or if she's curious. She seems too exhausted to be much of anything else right now. Maybe that's why I let the words slip out. Maybe this is the best possible timing.

"I want to learn more about Judaism," I offer by way of an explanation.

She sighs. "Did your grandfather put you up to this?"

"No," I say quickly. "I just . . . this whole funeral process really got me curious about the traditions. And the language. The music. All of it."

She gives me a look that says, *I don't believe you.*

"And I want to know more about our family's history," I say, knowing I'm picking at a fragile scab but unable to stop.

Mom stands up. "Not tonight, Rosie." She starts to leave the kitchen, shaking her head, as if I've done something cruel or thoughtless.

"Then when?" I say, more loudly than I thought it would come out.

She turns around and our eyes lock. "Some things are better left unknown," she says.

"It's too late," I say, not letting her look away. "I already know about Dahlia. I know Grandma was born in a displaced persons camp after the Holocaust. I know a lot of things, and I can't believe you never told me. I can't believe—"

Mom cuts me off with a look that's pure steel. "Not. Tonight."

She leaves. I'm alone in the fluorescent light of the kitchen. From the window I can see the sun setting, plunging the pool, the terrace, and of course the shed into darkness.

♪

Before all the sun's light can fade, I race outside. If Mom won't talk to me about all the things I want to know, I have to take advantage of the next-best thing. Or maybe Shanna is the *better* thing.

I've never been to the shed at night. It's only just after eight o'clock—not exactly late, but I don't know if Shanna will be there. I just have to hope.

I hear her before I see her, the notes of Grandma's song from Hungary coming from the walls of the shed. I don't know if Shanna is humming it or if the shed itself is radiating the melody. Now that I know it, I recognize it everywhere.

I burst through the door, out of breath from

running. I haven't planned what I'm going to say to Shanna, but as soon as I see her face, the words begin to tumble out.

"Do you know who I am?" I ask a startled Shanna.

She smiles hesitantly. "I'm pretty sure you're Rosie. Right?"

I shake my head. "I mean, yes, but that's not what I meant."

She seems wary, and after our last conversation I don't blame her. "What did you mean?"

"Who we are to each other," I say, taking another step into the shed, so that I can see the moon, full and bright, through the skylight.

"We're friends, aren't we?" Shanna asks. She looks more like my mother than ever in the semidarkness, which makes it easy to pencil in the lines around her eyes, the years of life, the changes of adulthood.

"Yes, we're friends," I say slowly. "And as your friend, I want to give you some advice."

Shanna snorts. "Like you did the other day? Telling me to magically find a way to play the violin *and* have a bat mitzvah?"

I grimace in embarrassment. "I'm sorry about that. It's just . . . there are some things I have to tell you."

Shanna folds her arms across her chest. "Well?"

I don't know where to begin, like I'm trying to find a bridge or chorus so I can jump into a piece of music. I take a deep breath and start with the first bit that I can put into words. "Don't be afraid to get another dog."

Shanna stares at me.

"You lost Stimpy, and it hurt. But don't let that keep you from loving something again. That goes for people too. Your parents, your sister . . ."

Shanna's eyes are wide.

"And you know how you said your biggest worry was losing your mom? Well, it's not going to happen anytime soon, but it will happen someday. So make sure to spend time with her—ask her questions while you can. Ask about her family. And spend time with your dad, because he's pretty great. You should try going swimming with him."

"What?" Shanna takes a step backward, away from me. "What are you talking about? How do you know my parents? How do you know my mom is going to live for a long time?"

I just keep going. "Oh! And there's a photo album, and some other stuff, in Europe. Lily's going to find it. It's your grandmother's stuff. You're going to want to see it. Let it mean something to you. Let it in. Like music—you have to let it all in. Don't try to keep everything—and everyone—out."

"Stop it," Shanna says. "You're scaring me again."

"Don't be scared. Or, actually, it's okay to be scared. Just don't let it stop you. Figure out what your dreams are and go after them."

Shanna backs up so far that she's against the thin wall of the shed. "Who are you?"

"I'm . . . we're related, okay? I'm part of your family. And I'm just trying to help."

Tears roll down Shanna's cheeks. "You're *not* helping."

"I don't know if it's too late," I say, tears filling my eyes too, "but if any of this changes how you live the next thirty years—if it makes you, or anyone you love, even a little happier—"

"Please don't tell me anything more," Shanna says. "I just want to go home."

I thought I'd feel a sense of satisfaction once I said what I wanted to say. But mostly I feel defeated. All I've done is upset her again.

I think she's going to run off crying, like she did last time. Instead, she lunges toward me, wrapping me in a tight, brief hug. There's music in it, and I wonder for a second if Shanna knows exactly who I am to her.

Before I have a chance to react, she walks through the door and out into the night.

♪

It's the last day of shiva, and no one has shown up yet. It's understandable: the neighbors have already dropped off more food than we can eat; friends from the synagogue have been over two or three times during the week. Dad left early in the morning to head back home. He has to get back to work. There are only so many surgeries his colleagues can cover.

In the late afternoon, Grandpa goes upstairs to rest and Aunt Lily goes to run some errands. So it's just Mom and me and Vienna, sitting in the quiet stillness of the sunroom.

I'm playing my conversation with Shanna from the night before over and over in my head, wondering if anything I said to her then could have an impact on my life now, when Mom clears her throat.

"I'm sorry I wasn't ready to talk last night when you brought up wanting to have a bat mitzvah," she says, looking out a window instead of at me.

"That's okay," I say, even though it's not, really.

"When I was your age," she says slowly and carefully, "I had a bat mitzvah. But I hated doing it. It felt like a lot of pressure. And there were other things I wanted to be doing. So I didn't want that for you."

I'm scared to say anything, in case I break the spell that has her talking to me like a real person.

She continues. "And I know you hate it when I say this, but I hope you'll take up the violin again when we get back home, so you probably won't have time for anything else. Plus, you'd be behind—other kids have been preparing for bar and bat mitzvahs for years, and you've never so much been to temple, let alone Hebrew school, so—"

"And whose fault is all that?" I stand up, surprising Vienna, who gets up and trots over to her dog bed, away from the tension. "You decided that the violin was the only thing I would ever do." I probably sound ungrateful, but I can't help it.

"I didn't choose this!" she cries, red now. "I didn't put this on you. You were born this way. I didn't ask for it, I'm just . . ." She looks around helplessly. "I'm just trying to make the most of it. For you. For the world!"

My mother is all the shades of red. She's high

notes and low notes, four hundred and forty vibra-tions a second. Deep and bright and hot and angry, but also vibrant and lively. I recognize this tone. This is the color she puts on when she wants to hide behind it.

"Do you know," she hisses in a low, bright red, the color of fresh blood, "when I was pregnant, I prayed, 'Just let it be easy. Just let her be normal.' But you're not. You have a gift. It's who you are. How could I possibly ignore it?"

"But you want to ignore other things about me," I tell her, speaking quietly in blue. I can't match her color when all I feel is sadness.

"I don't know what you mean by that." Mom shakes her head, and suddenly I hear it. She isn't just red. She never has been. This whole time, I've heard the wrong notes. My mother has all this blue just beneath the surface. She's been purple all along. Anger plus sadness is purple.

Purple is vivid and real and layered. Purple is what you are when you can sing two notes at once, when you hear harmony with every melody before you even learn the notes. Purple is what I've seen in Shanna's eyes sometimes. You sound purple if you've ever cried your eyes out at night. You're purple if you love someone who can't love you back the way you want to be loved—the way you need it.

"Mom," I say, matching her color perfectly, "do you . . ." I'm not sure I can say it. I wish I could paint it or play it on my violin. But sometimes, all you have are the words. "Mom," I start again, violet and lavender creeping in with softness. "Do you ever hear music in color?" I already know the answer. What I don't know is if Mom will be honest with me.

"Why do you ask that?"

My eyes fill with tears, because even though she hasn't answered yet, at least she hasn't shut me down. She's listening. She's *open*. That has to count for something. That has to be evidence of the thread connecting me to her, to Shanna. To Florence and Dahlia.

"Sometimes," I say slowly, inching toward her as if she's a wild animal and I'm trying not to frighten her off. "When someone hears music." I speak a little at a time, trying to make it sound safe. "They hear it in colors."

Mom steps closer to me too, but there's still so much space between us. "I think I know what you're saying. I . . ." She trails off, green and blue and purple in a braid of wispy smoke. "Maybe I did. Maybe

I did at one time. But I—I let go of all that. I didn't have a place for it in my life. My mother told me I sounded crazy when I talked about it. She told me people would think I was strange, and I didn't want to be strange. She told me never to mention it again, and I didn't."

I nod, worrying my bottom lip. *Is it something you can just decide to turn off?* I wonder.

"Do you?" she asks me quietly.

All I do is nod. I don't utter a sound. I have no idea what color would come out if I did. I feel exposed and raw.

I've gotten the answer I wanted, but it doesn't solve anything. She is who she is. And I am who I am. The tears spill over my eyes.

"Oh, Rosie!" She reaches toward me, even though we're still too far apart to touch. "It's different for you. You get to channel that ability in a way I never could. You have a gift."

"But shouldn't I be the one who gets to decide how to use it?"

She doesn't have a response for that. She just stares at me.

"I have to go," I say.

I need to talk to Shanna again.

CHAPTER 19

legato: smooth and connected

When I get to the shed, Shanna isn't there. That's okay. I can wait. She will come eventually.

I sit on the floor and watch the shadows move as the sun arches across the sky over the skylight.

I play through a Bach symphony in my head. I must nod off at one point, because I dream that Shanna is there, but when I wake, I'm still alone.

The sun has set, and she still hasn't come.

My stomach rumbles with hunger. I can see the moon through the skylight. Still no Shanna.

The tears start rolling down my cheeks before the thought crystalizes, but I hear it, like a song. *She's not coming back. She's gone.*

I have so many things I wanted to ask her. I want to apologize for bombarding her with weird life advice. I want to start over—I want to get to know her better.

I want, I want, I want.

All the sadness of losing Grandma Florence, of barely knowing her in the first place, of not having known my family's history until now, of spending my life playing the violin at the expense of everything else—it all pours out. I sob, alone in the shed, more certain with each passing second that I will never see Shanna again.

Which is why I don't hear the door creak open and am shocked when my mother steps inside.

"Rosie," she says with a pink softness in her voice I've never heard before. "Are you okay? We've been looking all over for you."

"I'm sorry," I whisper, still crying, not sure what I'm even sorry for. I'm curled up on the floor of the shed, my arms tucked around my knees.

"You missed the last shiva service, but it's okay," she tells me, still looming above me in her dress and heels.

This is the first time I've ever seen another person in this shed. Besides Shanna, besides me. And if Mom is here and Shanna isn't, it means that the circle has been connected. They can't both be here at the same time, of course. They're not two separate people.

Fresh tears spring to my eyes. I know for sure now that I've lost Shanna. There's no way to have them both.

"I'm sorry," I repeat.

Mom takes off her shoes, tucks her skirt around her legs, and sits on the shed floor. She puts a hand on my head, and my tears slow. I relax slightly.

"I used to come here a lot when I was a kid," she says, looking up at the skylight.

I look up too, studying her face for recognition. Because she may be Shoshanna now, but she's Shanna somewhere inside. "You did?"

She nods. "I imagined all kinds of stuff in here. It was like my own place. I can't believe it's still standing, actually."

She smiles, and I wonder what she's seeing in her mind. What she remembers. Whether anything actually got through. After all, if she once met a twelve-year-old girl named Golden Rose inside this shed, and now she's sitting here with her twelve-year-old daughter named Golden Rose, this would be the time to bring it up.

But she doesn't say anything else. My conversations

with Shanna must belong to some alternate dimension, some pocket of space-time that hasn't filtered into Mom's memories. Or maybe my Shanna *was* a different Shanna, one from a totally separate universe. Except she was the same in all the ways that mattered. And whether I changed her or not, she certainly changed me.

"Mom," I say after a long pause, "I'm sorry you lost your mom."

She looks down at me, her face softening, and I can almost see Shanna in her eyes. "Thank you," she says. "That's really sweet. I'm sorry you lost your grandma."

There's a long pause as we both look up at the moon.

"I got a text from your pool friends," she says after a while.

I sit up straight. I would've called them my library friends, or my improv friends, but I suppose Mom only knows them from that one time at the pool.

"That boy, Mason, texted that they're having a final performance for their improv camp class and he wanted to invite you. And me. He was very nice about it. Very appropriate."

I feel a smile spread across my lips, which is

surprising, considering that I was crying just a few minutes ago.

"I get what you like about him," Mom says.

I blush. She noticed his flippy hair and killer smile?

"I'm not saying *I* have any interest in him, silly. I just mean that I get it." Mom shifts and motions for me to come closer. To my surprise, she pulls me in so that my head is now on her lap. She begins playing with my hair. We used to sit like this, but I can't remember the last time we did. Maybe when I was five? Six at the most? Still, it feels familiar and safe and so, so lovely.

"Having a crush on a much older boy is understandable at your age," she says. "It's . . . safe. Because it's not actually going anywhere." She stops running her fingers through my hair. "Or, at least, it shouldn't go anywhere. We've talked about grooming and predatory relationships, and the power dynamic in age disparities, right?"

I laugh. "For the millionth time, yes, Mom."

She twirls my hair in her hands again.

"That's what it was," I say. "A safe crush. I'm pretty sure he's in love with Sunita anyway."

"But it can feel nice to have a crush like that,"

Mom says, nodding. "It's good practice for a real one."

"Ew," I say automatically. It's not that I don't want to have a crush for real, but I don't want to talk to my mom about it.

As if reading my mind, she says, "I guess you have Julianne to talk about that stuff with now."

I sit up, looking at her eye to eye again. "Seriously, thank you for telling her mom about Grandma Florence. That was really nice. I know you felt like Mrs. Farnsworth was mean to you back in the spring."

Mom sighs, and if I had my eyes closed, I would swear it was Shanna—the same girlish, mint-green wisp of a sigh. "I guess I realized it wasn't about me," she says. "Kind of like your violin strike."

I can't help it: I gasp.

"I took that really personally, like you were rejecting everything I'd done for you, everything I'd sacrificed for all these years. But maybe it wasn't . . about me."

I ease back into her lap, letting her play with my hair again. I can be more honest when I can't see her face. "Honestly, I didn't know how else to get your attention."

"So it *was* about me," she says, but not snarkily. As if she earnestly wants to know. Like Shanna would.

"Yes and no," I say, thinking it out in these terms for the first time. "It was also about *me*. I wanted to see who I was without the violin. Which I still don't know yet, to be honest. But I know I want to have more in my life than just playing violin."

"It's okay not to know who you are yet," Mom says gently. "I'm still working on that myself."

I sit up and face her again. "Really?"

She shrugs. "I think I put too much on you and the violin. I got a little lost, maybe, in managing your career. It's possible I lost . . . myself."

And there it is. Something I said to Shanna came through.

There's been a shift, however tiny, in the universe. *Shanna*, I think, *you heard me. And you did something.* She made a change, and I'm feeling its ripple effect.

I start crying all over again, because I know that this change in my mother, this softness, is from Shanna. I can't have both of them, but I hope I can keep the best of each of them.

Mom is crying too. "I'm sorry you felt like you

had to get my attention. I thought I was giving you all my attention, all the time."

"But not the kind I needed," I say through tears.

"I know," she murmurs, scooting me up to put her arms around me, letting me cry into her chest. "I'll try to do better."

There is so much more to say, but not right now. I'm tired and hungry, and for the first time in years, my mother is holding me like I'm a little kid, and I feel safe. I feel seen for who, not what, I am. I feel loved.

The next morning, I sleep in. Mom and I were at the shed pretty late, but she beats me to breakfast and is sitting there with Grandpa and Aunt Lily when I come down.

"Good morning!" Grandpa says, and I lean over to hug him. I saw on my way down the stairs that our mirrors have been uncovered. The first part of the mourning period is over. It doesn't feel like things are back to the way they were, but like we're starting a new chapter. Everything is different but we're all in it together.

"Ready for our walk around the block?" Aunt Lily asks.

I look from her to Mom to Grandpa, wondering what Lily means.

"At the end of shiva," Grandpa explains, "some people take a walk around their neighborhood to symbolize that they're ready to rejoin the world."

I nod. "I like that." And I do feel ready, in a strange way, to rejoin the world. As if I've been traveling, and I'm ready to go home.

"It'll be good for me to get reacquainted with the area," Aunt Lily says as I grab a muffin from a basket in front of Grandpa.

"Does this mean it's happening?" Mom asks.

There's another moment of silence as they all grin, and I have to ask, "What?"

"I'm moving here," Aunt Lily says. "I'm going to keep your grandpa company."

Mom laughs. "And out of trouble."

"I don't get into trouble," Grandpa protests.

Mom pats his hand. "Well, I won't have to worry as much now."

"But what about Austria?" I blurt out. "What about your job?"

Aunt Lily looks down at her plate, suddenly busy

eating eggs. "Well, there are a lot of things I'll miss about Austria," she says. "But I can work remotely these days, and . . ." Her voice wavers. "It's time for me to come home."

My eyes are wide as I look to each of them, trying to piece together what must've changed to make this arrangement happen. Perhaps a ripple through time, a strand of something from another dimension.

"Your mother finally asked for some help," Grandpa says in a teasing tone. He's talking to me but looking at his daughters.

"I'm happy to help," Lily says.

Mom looks at her sister. "And I'm happy to have you living a little closer again."

Lily's eyes fill with tears. "I missed a lot over the years. I don't want to miss even more."

She and Mom are both crying now, and Grandpa looks at me as if to say, "Can you believe these two?" but there are tears in his eyes too.

Later, I ask Mom how she convinced Lily to move home, and why Lily had stayed away for so long in the first place.

Mom stops folding her clean laundry and looks at me. "There's a lot of history you don't know. And some of it isn't mine to share. The rest of it . . ."

She trails off and I pick up a shirt to fold. I'm not great at folding, and I know Mom is going to redo my attempts, but I need something to do with my hands.

"Well, I heard you the other day," she goes on. "About wanting to know more about our family's history, about Judaism. And I'm going to work on that."

I nod. "Cool," I say, like it's no big deal, even though it means a lot. I feel like this olive branch she's extending deserves something from me in return, so I gather up my courage and say, "Mom, I played the violin for Grandma before she died."

Mom drops the clothing she's been folding. "You did?"

I nod. "Is that okay?"

She picks up the laundry again and starts refolding. "Did you do it because you wanted to?" She's looking past me, like she can't quite meet my eyes, like this is hard for her.

"Yeah," I said.

"Then I'm glad," she says. "I'm really glad."

CHAPTER 20

duet: a piece of music written for
two performers

We all go to the improv class show. Grandpa, Aunt Lily, Mom, and I pile into Mom's car and head to the library on Friday afternoon. Mom and I are driving back to Maryland tomorrow, so the timing is perfect.

The performance is outside, where there's a wooden platform stage with about a hundred folding chairs facing it. It's cooler than it was the week of the pool incident, but still a little too hot to be completely comfortable.

"I'm already sweating," Aunt Lily murmurs as we find seats near the back.

Grandpa looks at his watch. "How long is this thing going to be?"

I bite the insides of my cheeks to keep from laughing. Mom and I told them a million times that they did not have to come, but they both insisted it would be good for the other to get "out and about." It's a little peek into what their life is going to be like, living together, taking care of each other. I hope it means I'll get to see them both a lot more often.

I feel a little embarrassed as I scan the seats and realize that, somewhere in the crowd, Mason's parents are probably there. And Sunita's, and Ryan's, and Francie's, and Taylor's. The last thing I want is for Mom to talk to them about the pool incident. I suddenly wish we hadn't come.

But when the show starts, I change my mind. It's kind of uneven—some scenes are really funny, and others feel like inside jokes I don't get. But I can tell the performers are having a good time. I remember a few of the things Mia taught them during the classes I watched, and it's neat to see those things being played out on stage.

The show is pretty short, and when it's over, Grandpa and Aunt Lily both say they're glad they came.

Mom looks over at me and smiles, asking, "Do you want to say hi to your friends?"

I don't. I'm full of shame about the last time I saw them, about how it ended. But Sunita spots me when the performers join the audience. She runs over to me, and I'm glad I didn't just slink away.

"Thank you for coming!" she squeals.

"You did a great job," I say.

Mason walks up. "You came!" He reaches out his hand for a fist bump and I oblige.

"Thanks for texting my mom," I say, feeling like a little kid. But Mason flashes his heart-stopping smile at me and I feel like it was all worth it.

I look over at Mom, who nods permission. So I follow Mason and Sunita over to where Ryan, Francie, and Taylor are gathered with some other kids from the class. They all greet me with high-fives and fist bumps, and I tell them all I'm headed home tomorrow.

"We'll keep an eye out for your YouTube videos," Ryan says.

I look at him in confusion. "My what?"

Ryan smiles, showing his perfectly straight, white teeth. "We all know you're a violin star. It's only a matter of time before you give a fancy concert where the whole thing is recorded and uploaded to the internet, and we'll say, 'Oh my gosh, we know her!' and we'll brag about being friends with you to all our other friends."

I don't know what to say. It's possibly one of the nicest things anyone has said to me. "Thanks," I manage finally. "We'll see."

"You're going to play again, though, right?" Taylor asks, in their blunt-but-kind way.

"Yeah," Francie says. "You were really, really good when you played my viola. You have to keep making music, Rosie."

I look back behind me, where my family is waiting patiently, talking to each other by the parking lot.

"I think I will find a way," I tell my friends. I hug each of them goodbye. Mason is last. It's over in a flash—Mom would be happy it's a very "appropriate" hug—but I take in the way his arms feel on mine and his sweaty, spicey, deodorant smell, and the music radiating off of him the way my mind sees him.

"Goodbye," I say to them all. "Thanks for letting me hang out with you a little bit this summer."

I wonder, as I walk over to my family, if I'll ever see any of them again. But time is a circle. I'll never forget them, or this summer, and in that way, I will see them again in my mind anytime I want to. In a way, nothing is ever over. No one is ever gone. *Goodbye* is just a word we say when we get to a repeat sign, and then we go back to the beginning and look for the coda.

♪

We only have a few hours left at the house before Mom and I drive back home, and I have so many things I need to do.

One of the hardest is finding a way to say good-bye to Vienna. I don't know how I'm going to let go of that shaggy, smelly, wonderful dog. I think back to the beginning of the summer, when I was scared of her, when I thought the world would end if she slobbered on me. Now, I'd let her sleep in my bed with me if she wanted to.

I'm lying on the floor, my arm thrown over Vienna's coarse coat, when Grandpa enters the sun-room and almost steps on us.

"Sorry, Grandpa," I say, as he startles and steps back.

Grandpa smiles. "There you are! I was looking for you."

I sit up, and Grandpa slowly squats down so we're eye to eye.

"I have a favor to ask of you," he says. His eyes are a little cloudy. I don't know if that's from age or from all the emotions of the past few weeks. "I was hoping you'd take this here dog home with you for a while." He rubs Vienna's belly but keeps looking right at me.

"You want me to take Vienna back to Baltimore? To live with me?" I ask in disbelief.

Grandpa nods. "She's a little much for me to take care of these days. And your aunt Lily isn't . . . a big fan, should we say?"

I haven't really noticed Lily being one way or another toward Vienna, but I can imagine that taking care of a dog on top of all the other changes happening in her life might be a bit much.

"I would love it, Grandpa, but Mom would never let me."

He grins, which makes me realize he wouldn't have made this offer before talking to Mom. "Why don't you go ask her yourself?"

Mom is in the living room. Her smile makes me suspect that she's not just in on this, but that she's behind all of it.

"Can we really bring Vienna home?" I ask her, tears welling up in my eyes for the millionth time.

Mom shrugs. "I think it'd be good for us to have a pet. To teach you responsibility."

At that, we all laugh—Mom, Grandpa, and I. I've already had way too much responsibility, but I appreciate Mom's sense of humor about it.

"You'll have to agree to feed and walk her," Mom tells me.

"I will!" I exclaim, thinking back to Shanna and the shed, and Stimpy, and Mom's previous stance on dogs. Time is a circle, isn't it?

I look at Grandpa, a thought occurring to me. "But won't you miss her?" I ask.

Grandpa puts an arm around me, squeezing me tight. "Aunt Lily and I will just have to come visit you all the time, won't we?"

"Will you?" I can't remember the last time my grandparents came to Maryland.

"That's one of the benefits of having Lily live here," Mom explains. "She can drive Grandpa down any time."

I wrap my arms around Grandpa. "Thank you," I whisper into his chest. "For Vienna. And for everything."

Before I can get too emotional, Mom gasps, and I quickly pull apart from Grandpa to see why.

"I just realized," she says solemnly, "that my car is going to be covered in dog hair."

Grandpa and I try not to laugh. We really do, but it's hard to keep it in.

Mom buries her face in her hands. "Oh, what have I agreed to?" she moans melodramatically, even as she joins in our laughter.

"What am I missing?" calls Aunt Lily, coming in from the dining room. She's holding the viola case.

Mom shakes her head, wiping her eyes. "Oh, nothing much. I'm just realizing I'm going to have to be a little less uptight if I'm going to be a dog person."

Aunt Lily makes a teasing face. "You? Less uptight? That's going to be a process!"

Mom looks at me. "I'm working on it."

Lily holds out the viola case to me. "I believe this is yours," she says.

Before I take it, I ask everyone to wait for a minute.

I run into Mom's room, Vienna trailing behind me, and find my violin in her closet, where it's been almost the entire summer, except for the times I brought it upstairs.

I carry it to the living room and hold it out to Mom. "I want you to have this," I say.

Mom frowns. "Are you quitting for good?"

I set the violin down and take the viola case from Aunt Lily. "Well, I can't play two instruments at once, can I?"

Mom looks from me to Aunt Lily—who raises her hands in a *don't look at me* gesture—to Grandpa, who smiles.

"If anyone could," Grandpa says, "it would be you, my Golden Rose."

This makes me feel so warm and happy inside. But I tell all three of them, "I'm ready for a change. I'm going to play the viola. I want to be the harmony for a while, not the melody."

They're all silent, just listening to me.

"I can use all my technical skills from the violin, but I can start something new. Something that's mine. Something I chose."

I think of Dahlia, and I wonder if I did choose the viola. Or if some of who I am is written in my DNA, passed down from generation to generation, inscribed with the knowledge and trauma and experiences of those who came before me.

I look at Mom. "I think *you* should play the

violin," I tell her gently. I wonder if, somehow, somewhere, she hears an echo, because I've said this to her before.

"I want you to take over one of my lessons with Agnieszka each week," I say. If this plan is going to work, I'm going to need to spend less time on music-related activities. If I'm going to have a real life—with a dog to walk and a best friend to hang out with, The Garden of Fairy books to catch up on, and maybe an improv class of my own to take someday and a boy my age to have a crush on—I have to let something go. Also, a tiny, mischievous piece of me wants to see Mom struggle with Agnieszka's intensity and perfectionism. But only a tiny piece.

"I always did want to play an instrument," Mom says slowly, as if she's seriously considering it. There's a spark of longing in her eyes I recognize from Shanna.

"We could play a duet someday," I suggest, hoping this isn't too much for her.

She squeezes my hand. "I would like that."

In the car on the way home, Mom and I make up rules. This time, I sit up front, next to her, instead of in the back like I did on the drive up to Connecticut.

I write down the rules in a notebook as we come up with the list together. "I get to have a dog," I suggest as the first rule.

"Agreed," says Mom, getting onto the highway. "That one we've established."

I look behind me at the back seat, where Vienna is curled up among some of our suitcases and bags, sleeping happily.

I didn't know how she was going to say goodbye to Grandpa. Or how *I* was going to say goodbye to him, after all these weeks of becoming so close to him. But it was surprisingly easy, because Aunt Lily promised they'll come visit us in two weeks. Two weeks! That's nothing. That makes it way less hard.

"Rule Number Two," Mom says, "is that you get to decide which orchestras and concerts and symphonies you'll take part in."

I almost ask her to repeat herself so I can be super-sure I'm hearing her correctly. But we've talked about this one enough in the past twelve hours that I know it's real. I write it down.

"Rule Number Three is that I email Grandpa at least once a week," I say.

Before we left, Aunt Lily promised she's going to help him with email so he can write back to me.

"That's a great rule," Mom says, smiling over at me while keeping her eyes on the road.

"How about Rule Number Four is that Julianne and I have sleepovers at least once a month?" I ask. I haven't run this one by Julianne yet, but I love the idea of it and I'm hoping she will too.

"And Rule Number Five is that half of those sleepovers are at Julianne's house, so your dad and I can go out on a date sometimes," Mom adds.

I raise my eyebrows. "I like this one," I say.

"And Number Six is that you have to get ten hours of sleep on weeknights. No staying up late practicing the violin—I mean, viola."

I do not write this down. "Ten hours? Mom, how old do you think I am, seven? How about eight hours?"

"We'll look it up. Whatever you're supposed to get. Just no more staying up all night practicing. Right?"

"Right."

We fall into an easy silence, as the sound of the car speeding over the road mixes with the classical station playing Baroque string quartets. Vienna's breathing rounds it all out into the perfect sonata of road trip noise.

Before we left Grandpa's house, I went down to the shed one last time. I knew Shanna wouldn't be there—I knew it in my bones. But I wanted to see it one last time, and to leave something there for her in case she came back.

I wrote out the song from Hungary for her. Just in case she ever wants to play it. It felt like a fitting way to say thank you.

A while later, Mom says, "Number Seven," and I snap out of my daydream and pick up the pencil.

"Ready," I say.

"Rule Number Seven," she says slowly, "is that I'm going to listen to you more. I'm going to ask more questions, and really listen to your answers."

"Thanks, Mom," I say quietly. I don't write it down, though. I don't need to. "Rule Number Eight is that I'll do the same."

She takes one hand from the steering wheel and briefly squeezes mine.

"Rule Number Nine," I say. "Hebrew school."

She laughs. "Fine. I'm in favor of it if that's what you want."

I think about the connection I felt at Grandma's funeral and the untold stories I could feel in the photo albums. "That's what I want," I say. "And possibly a bat mitzvah."

"You have a lot of catching up to do if you want one by the time you turn thirteen," Mom says.

"Can't I do it when I'm fourteen?" I ask. "Or fifteen? If I need more time to learn?"

Mom considers this. A few raindrops splatter on the window and she turns on her windshield wipers. "Now that I think about it, I don't see why not. We don't have to be in any rush."

Time is a circle. It doesn't matter if I have a bat mitzvah when I'm thirteen or thirty. I'll get there.

♪

Julianne is waiting for us when we pull into the driveway at home. Mom let me use her phone to text Julianne when we were close, and she's biked over.

We squeal and jump up and down and hug each other like we haven't seen each other in years.

"I can't believe you have a dog!" Julianne exclaims, petting Vienna as she lumbers out of the back seat and stretches.

"She probably needs to pee," I say, and Julianne lets Vienna amble over to some grass. We did stop at a rest stop along the way to let Vienna eat and walk around and relieve herself, but it was still a long trip.

"Can I help you walk her? And feed her?" Julianne asks.

I nod. "Any time. She can be like your dog too."

Julianne links her arm with mine as we each carry a bag up to the front porch. "Oh, this is going to be fun," she says.

I couldn't agree more.

EPILOGUE

Da Capo: from the beginning

The next summer, I return. This time, though, it's my choice, and I bring my viola. I practice in the mornings because I want to, not because I have to. I bring Vienna, and she's happy to run in the huge yard around the house where she used to live, but she stays close to me, because she knows that when I leave, she'll go with me. Her home is where I am now.

Grandpa Jack is glad we're here. He says Aunt Lily has been going overboard with her cooking experiments and with us there, he'll get to eat some "normal food." I'm happy Dad came along this time too.

It takes me three days to gather the courage to visit the shed. I know Shanna won't be there. I understand that we can truly never meet again. But

I left her the music I wrote, and I want to see if she left me anything in return.

The brown mustiness of the shed, the door's silver squeak, the pink auras in the skylight are all just as they were last summer. Inside, it's still, and I feel the emptiness shimmer like an overture. It's gold and soft, and I see that the sheet music I left is gone. But in its place is a canvas, about three feet tall. It faces the wall, leaning up against it, and when I turn it around, I almost cry.

She painted the music I left for her. The sheet music I wrote out, treble clefs and grace notes, quarter rests and triplets—the way normal people read music—has been transposed into a painting. Exquisite turquoise brush strokes, with blush tones and streaks of gold. It's precise, it's every note of the song from Hungary. Melody over harmonies, layers and layers of acrylics on canvas. Every instrument of the symphony.

"Shanna," I say, although I know she isn't there, "it's perfect." I know she's gone now, but my mother is waiting back at the house for me, completely unaware of the painting or the colors or the music, yet finally ready to hold me in her arms and love me, exactly as I am.

Questions for Discussion

1. Seeing colors is one of the ways Rosie interprets sound. What are some moments in the story where the colors stood out to you? How did Rosie feel? How did you feel?

2. Rosie takes a break from playing the violin partly because she's tired of it defining her identity. What other activities and interests does she discover over the course of the summer?

3. What draws Rosie to Shanna even before she realizes Shanna is her mom? What do you think makes Shanna want to befriend Rosie?

4. What do Grandpa Jack and Rosie's daily routines mean for them? How does their relationship change over the course of the story?

5. Throughout the book, Rosie observes Mia's improv class. What does she notice while watching the students perform and interact? How is this

different from the environments where Rosie is used to spending time?

6. After seeing her swim, Rosie's dad thinks she should pursue it competitively. Why does this hurt her?

7. How was Rosie's great-grandmother Dahlia affected by her experiences during the Holocaust? How did that trauma affect her daughter, Grandma Florence? What were its ripple effects for later generations of the family?

8. How does Rosie feel when she finally plays the song from Hungary for Grandma Florence? What does she realize about herself and her relationship to music?

9. Rosie hasn't been reliably present, physically or emotionally, to support Julianne during their friendship. How do she and Julianne move past the ways Rosie hurt Julianne? When you want to make amends for hurting someone, what do you do?

10. What does Rosie learn about her mother over the course of the novel? What does Rosie learn about herself?

Author's Note

I loved writing this book at this unique time in my life when I am firmly in the middle generation of my family, actively both a mother and a daughter. I had an unusual childhood, and while it was nothing like Rosie's and I wasn't exactly a prodigy like she is, I did find some professional success early in life, before most of my peers knew what they wanted to do and to be. I wanted to tell a story about what that kind of childhood can be like. I wasn't that kid, but I definitely knew those kids. And those parents.

Of course, this is a work of fiction. I'm fortunate that my parents, unlike Rosie's, made sure I was well-rounded and had as many typical childhood and family experiences as possible, as well as full knowledge of and experiences in our Jewish culture, faith, and history. While I used family names for a few characters, including Florence and Jack, no character in this book is based on anyone from real life.

Hawthorne, Connecticut, isn't a real town, though it's inspired by my own childhood summers and the people, places, and dogs that shaped me.

It was an extra joy to write about music for this book. For many years, music was a major part of my life both personally and professionally. But since my mid-twenties, I'd had a hard time finding as much space for music. Like Rosie, I always hear it playing inside my brain, but I'd devoted less time to truly enjoying music, to listening to it on purpose, or to singing or playing, until I started working on this book.

I wanted to write about synesthesia because I have it myself. Synesthesia links or blends usually unrelated sensory experiences. Basically, input that would stimulate only one sense (such as hearing) for most people can activate multiple senses at once (such as both hearing and sight) for someone with synesthesia. There are many, many types of synesthesia, and even people with the same type may experience it differently. Rosie's synesthesia is different from mine, and that is purposeful—this isn't an autobiography!—but it was fun to extrapolate from my own neurodivergence to tap into Rosie's. I didn't realize quite how atypical my brain is until adulthood. So I hope neurodivergent kids reading this book see familiar things in Rosie, and I hope all my readers take away a sense of the beauty in all the different ways our minds can work. There is no one way to be, no one way to experience the world. You should never have to be afraid to share what makes you different, because I promise it makes you the strongest and best version of yourself. And no matter what, you are enough.

Any book I write is bound to have some pieces of Judaism and Jewish life in it, because that is my own culture. But I didn't initially realize what a big part Judaism would come to play in this story. As I wrote it, the United States was experiencing a time of particularly intense antisemitism, and I found myself wanting to talk more about my family's Judaism: how it's shaped our history, how it continues to echo through the generations, and how beautiful and special the traditions are.

My grandmother, the real Florence, was lucky enough to be born in the United States, but most of her extended family members were killed by the Nazis during the Holocaust. We have a short piece of black-and-white film showing them before the war—the last time her cousins and aunts and uncles were all together—and to this day, watching it makes me feel incredibly sad. However, while I was writing this book, a distant relative got in touch with my sister to share that his grandmother was Florence's first cousin—and that, unbeknownst to us, she had survived the Holocaust and was still alive in Israel. (She has since passed away, at the age of ninety-six!) This renewed my fascination with the ways our families were splintered and fractured, and the modern miracle that happens when we can connect, even after all this time.

Acknowledgments

This book is dedicated to my parents, Andy and Toba Barth. I am so grateful to them for raising me, teaching me, and giving me incredible opportunities. Thank you for being nothing like any of the parents in this book! Also, I am lucky to have another set of parents who have helped raise me since I was nineteen: my parents-in-law, Bob and Sue Isler. Thank you for loving me as your own!

After publishing my first book, the middle grade novel *AfterMath*, all I wanted was the chance to write and publish more. This book is a dream come true.

To my sister, Ellen Barth: your research into our family history was inspiring and immeasurably helpful to this story and to me. I'm so glad I have a sibling to do life with—and especially grateful that it is YOU!

My agent, Emily S. Keyes, has been with me every step of the way in this book's process. She has encouraged me and tolerated my billions of emails with subject lines like, "Is this anything?" She has strategized and brainstormed with me and made me laugh. Writing can be lonely at times, but having Emily in my corner has made it so much more fun. #TheEmilys

If you've had a conversation with me over the past four or five years, I've definitely told you how much I love my editor, Amy Fitzgerald. She is uniquely talented and brilliant, teaching me how to be a better storyteller with every single conversation, note, and suggestion. Amy, thank you for hearing the words "generational trauma" and responding with "I love this plan!" as the focus of this book evolved. You are such a gift in my life, and I LOVE working with you. Thanks for never shying away from the hard/sad/weird with me!

To the whole team at Carolrhoda/Lerner, including Danielle Carnito, Erica Johnson, Mandi Andrejka, and especially Lindsay Matvick and Megan Ciskowski, who have helped me so much to connect with more readers! Annie Zheng, I can't thank you enough for your insights! Jieting Chen, thank you for the gorgeous cover illustration! You captured the story so beautifully, I can almost hear it like a song!

A huge thanks to the other writers (and friends) in my life who have kept me sane and creative and hopeful with their encouragement and stories and notes, and whose work has also inspired me greatly: Rachel Axler, Jennifer Jackson, Amanda Deibert Staggs, Jen McCreary, Stephen James, Nora Zelevansky, Hanna Neier, Katie Schorr, Kate Spencer, Gwen Mesco, Mandi Palley, Jessica Eason, Samara Bay, Sharon Levin, Kelli Midgley, Yona Zeldis McDonough, Judith Viorst, Wendy Molyneux, Jeff Drake, Lynn Chen, Jimmy Matejek-Morris, Oona Hanson, Jennifer Chen, Erin McAnoy, Susie Mendoza, Miellyn Fitzwater Barrows, Katie Davis Reich, Edith Cohn, Eirene Tran Donohoe, Kate Sweeney, and the whole Write x3 group.

A special shout-out to Amy Preiser Maoz, who is always there to brainstorm or commiserate or inspire or share, who has given me so much as a friend and as a writer. I love you!

Thank you to the wonderful authors who've blurbed this book: Barbara Dee, Gail Lerner, Joanne Levy, Jimmy Matejek-Morris, Sally J. Pla, and Elly Swartz.

Thanks to my extended family: Ellen, Brian, Leo, and Felix; Tom, Lavanya, and Jayani; Amy,

Omry, Nate, and Ben; Susannah, Douglas, Abigail, Jonathan, Rachel, Barbara, Eric, Nancy, Michael, Flora, Laslo, Frank, Nada; all the Barths, Wolfs, Gaucks, Weisses, Dobkins, Boyds, Islers, Strongs, Friedmanns, Oznicks, Hamiltons, Kondapallis; and the Cricket Buddies, Rebecca Gifford Goldberg and Jenny Lang.

I am lucky to have a bunch of people in my life who believe in me and thus make it possible for me to keep writing and telling stories: Ryan Cunningham, Cindy Ambers, Spencer Robinson, Susanne Norwitz, Terri Hall, Kate Sandoval Box, Elizabeth Blye, Regan Chagal, Jordan Scott, the Tosh family, Rachel Hamilton, Caryn Gorden, and The Pile.

All my love and gratitude to Jim, Hallie, and Max—my biggest fans, my three true loves, the most important people to me. I love you each so much. Thanks for being my family and for putting up with the times when I completely disappeared into writing this book.

About the Author

Emily Barth Isler is an author of essays and children's books, including the middle grade novel *AfterMath*. She lives in Los Angeles, California, with her husband and their two kids. Find her at www.emilybarthisler.com.

Praise for
AfterMath

"This book is a gift to the culture."

—Amy Schumer, writer, actor, and activist

"Lucy's story of grief and healing packs an emotional punch that will tug at your heartstrings long after you've read the last page."

—Edith Cohn, author of *Birdie's Billions*

"*AfterMath* is gorgeously written, infinitely heart-wrenching, and tragically timely. Lucy's voice is powerful and distinct. I loved this novel."

—Leslie Margolis, author of *Ghosted*, *We Are Party People*, and the Maggie Brooklyn Mysteries

"*AfterMath* is both heartbreaking and filled with hope. Gentle, nuanced, and honest, Isler's extraordinary debut will stay with readers long beyond the final page."

—Alex Richards, author of *Accidental*

"This novel comes pretty close to perfect in its fearless and compassionate exploration of the sorrows, struggles, and hard-won maturing of a spunky twelve-year-old as she deals with loss. The losses are real, the pain is real, but so—the author persuades us—is the saving grace of loving connection."

—Judith Viorst, author of *The Tenth Good Thing about Barney*

"This book is for any kid who has ever felt alone with pain. It offers a light, an understanding, a togetherness that brings hope."

—Melissa Walker, author of *Why Can't I Be You*

"Emily Barth Isler handles so many potentially explosive topics with grace and subtlety but also with enormous assurance and power. This is a brave, important and even essential novel."

—Yona Zeldis McDonough, author of *The Bicycle Spy* and *Courageous*